HOW TO OUTRUN A CROCODILE WHEN YOUR SHOES ARE UNTIED

JESS KEATING

sourcebooks
jabberwocky

Published by Sourcebooks Jabberwocky, an imprint of Sourcebooks, Inc.
P.O. Box 4410, Naperville, Illinois 60567-4410
(630) 961-3900
Fax: (630) 961-2168
www.jabberwockykids.com

Library of Congress Cataloging-in-Publication data is on file with the publisher.

Source of Production: Versa Press, East Peoria, Illinois, USA
Date of Production: April 2014
Run Number: 5001367

Printed and bound in the United States of America.
VP 10 9 8 7 6 5 4 3 2

To everyone trying to find their bravest, truest self.

Warning: This book contains real-life situations and stuff that has actually happened to me. I'm talking lots of awful boy behavior, wretched girls, best friends who are missing in action, and ridiculous amounts of elephant poop. This book is not for the faint of heart, or anybody who has recently had a big meal or is suffering from a heinous zit anywhere in the chin region. Oh, and don't read it if you're afraid of snakes. I mean, you shouldn't be afraid of snakes, because they're really nice animals and not at all as terrible as their bad reputations make them out to be. But still.

—*Ana Wright, Anonymite Extraordinaire*

chapter 1

Rattlesnakes are born without rattles.
                                    —*Animal Wisdom*

That's sort of sad, isn't it? I mean, what good is a baby without a rattle? Not that snakes are cute at the best of times, but is that their fault?

Don't. Freak. *Out.*

It was the day before my twelfth half-birthday, and I was spending it holding the business end of a crocodile.

That's the end *without* the teeth, by the way. But it can be just as dangerous and infinitely smellier.

"Just keep a nice firm grip with your legs, kiddo," Mike said. Mike is the head keeper in the Crocodile

Pavilion of the city's Zoological Park and Gardens. He was sitting on the end with teeth. At nine feet long with black, beady eyes, Louie was a favorite here, but Mike said he hadn't been eating his food like a good little reptile. That meant that the zoo staff had to wrangle him, secure him to this surfboard contraption, weigh him, and then feed him gross-looking brown liquid with a tube. All while making sure *we* didn't become dinner in the process.

Delightful.

"Okay, everybody," Mike said. "We've got the feeding tube secure. Graham is going to pump some food into him now, so just hang tight." His voice was calm and assertive, the exact opposite of my heart, which was dancing around like a Mexican jumping bean on a sugar rush.

Please, let this be quick.

I gripped my legs tighter on the thick, grayish-green scales. The rough sides of Louie's stomach expanded in and out, like a breathing rock. I knew Mike and his crew were only letting me help because my mom asked them. See, my parents (both zoologists) work at the zoo. Instead of playing video games or hanging out at the mall like regular, *normal* kids, my brother, Daz, and I spend most of our extra time mucking around behind the scenes, cleaning up elephant poop or counting crickets or tossing fish heads to penguins. You know, glamorous stuff.

Daz loves it because he gets to feed his favorite animals, the snakes. Something about watching the crickets get snapped up makes him cackle like a witch over a cauldron. He also has snakes at home—seventeen to be exact, including an ancient boa named Oscar that he constantly hides in my bed to freak me out. He's living the reptile dream.

Which, let's face it, is more of a nightmare for anyone who thinks animals should have those pesky things called "legs."

A bead of sweat worked its way down the back of my neck. The humidity was always suffocating in the pavilion, and with the hot May sun streaming through the skylights, I felt like an army of itchy ants was crawling all over me. I dipped my head, secretly trying to blow a stream of cool air down the front of my brown uniform. This was one time my glaring lack-of-chesticles was a good thing, but even my superlame training bra was itchy on my skin. I was just glad no one from school was here to see me, frizzy haired and sweating up a stink storm on the back of a reptile. Easy, breezy, beautiful crocodile girl.

As Graham was feeding the disgusting brown goop to Louie, I peeked down at my watch.

Seven minutes.

3

My fingers drummed against Louie's tail. I had seven minutes to ditch this crocodile and make it to the break room where my laptop was waiting. My chest tightened as I watched Mike take down measurements. Seven minutes until my life would be back to normal. Until everything would be on its way to being *right* again.

Hurry uuuuup.

I had to make it in time. I just *had* to. My eyelids fluttered closed, picturing the look on Liv's face when she heard my amazing idea. Who would have thought a cupcake could fix everything? And what perfect timing, with my half-birthday being tomorrow?

It had to be fate.

Ever since we were six and a half years old, my best friend, Livia, and I haven't missed a single half-birthday. We've made a wish on every one and have a pact to do it every year until we die. Last year, we wished for rollerblades on Liv's eleventh half-birthday and got them. My half-birthday before that was for tickets to see *West Side Story*, our second favorite musical, after *Les Misérables*, of course. Got that too. Liv says half-birthdays are even more important than regular birthdays because that's when you're at the highest point of your "birthday year," so you get the most amount of magic from your wish.

Ana and Livia's Rules of Half-Birthday Wishing are simple:

1. We have to wear the special homemade chocolate lip gloss that we made on her last half-birthday, so we can smell extra nice for the cupcake we're wishing on.
2. We both have to bite our cupcakes at the exact same time. No cheating.
3. We both have to wish for the same thing. This gives the wish *double* magic and helps it come true faster.

Usually, it's easy to do all this. But this time things are a lot more difficult. In fact, they're almost impossible.

That's because four days, seven hours, and forty-three minutes ago, Liv moved to New Zealand.

And I mean the *actual* New Zealand. With the sheep and the hobbits.

In geography terms, that's 7,968 miles away from me in Denver. In best friendship terms, it's just totally sucky. Why did her dad have to take that stupid job, anyway? There are plenty of jobs around in *this* country. This is why our wish this year had to be worth it.

It has to work.

It was our only chance.

In exactly five minutes, I was going to tell Liv what we should wish for this year.

Just as soon as I got off this crocodile.

"Only a little longer, guys. Everyone's doing great. Last-minute blood sample and we'll be done," Mike said, keeping an eagle eye on Louie's wrapped snout. A surge of pins and needles ran through my leg as I shifted on my knees. Not only was I roasting, now my butt had fallen asleep.

Four more minutes.

Right now, Liv would be loading up her video chat and clicking on my name. I couldn't stop the trembles of anticipation in my toes.

"Great work, people," Mike said, snapping me out of my daydream. "Food is done. Measurements are looking good. Dale is going to go around and untie all the roping, and we will all jump off when I say. Kiddo, I want you to shimmy right back to the tip of his tail. You'll be safest there, and Ben can move back to cover you," he said.

The three men on Louie's back nodded, shifting their weight to prepare. I scooted back, resting my weight on the heels of my boots. My butt and left leg ached.

Two minutes 'til I talk to her.

"All right, three," Mike said.

"Two." Everyone took a deep breath.

"*One.*"

We all leaped and dodged away from Louie's back, with Ben grabbing my shoulders to steer me out of trouble's way. With the ropes gone, Louie ambled away to his pool instantly, leaving the rest of us to sigh with relief. Mike beamed at me and clapped his clipboard against his palm. "Awesome job, kiddo. Not bad for your first croc wrangling, huh?"

I tried to force a smile on my face, but my heart was pounding in my ears. Mike didn't know I was about a minute away from saving my entire best friend future.

"Thanks, Mike," I said, hurrying to follow him through the heavy door out of the exhibit. "Maybe next time I'll take the end with teeth." I grimaced.

"You'll be a pro soon enough. You can be the star of the zoo!" He winked.

"Heh, maybe," I mumbled, scooting away.

Over my dead body.

One minute to go.

The break room of the Crocodile Pavilion was empty when I rushed through the door. I had thirty seconds left. I couldn't keep the smile from my face as I jerked open my laptop on the table and clicked frantically.

Liv's face burst onto my screen as a beaming mess

7

of pixels. She looked small next to the pile of boxes and furniture scattered around her new room.

"Hey!" she exclaimed in a tinny voice. Liv never wore a watch, but that didn't stop her from checking her wrist dramatically and clucking her tongue. "You're late." Her nose scrunched up like it always did when she was joking.

I wiped my sweaty forehead with my sleeve. "I know, I'm sorry. I was on the back of a crocodile," I said.

"Some things never change." She crossed her arms over her chest and fiddled with the tip of her blond hair.

I settled into my chair and pulled the laptop closer. It was so good to see Liv's face, even though it reminded me how much I missed her. It was just *wrong* for a best friend to move away. Like pouring orange juice on your cereal wrong. "So listen," I started. "I figured it out. I figured it *all* out!"

Liv's eyebrows lifted. "You finally discovered what that disgusting smell is in Daz's room? Was I right?" Her blue eyes twinkled deviously. "Was it a sacrifice to the Annoying Brother Gods? Is he now their king?"

I shook my head. "No! This is serious! I'm pretty sure he is their king, though. But really. I figured out what we need to wish for tomorrow! And I can't believe we didn't think of it until now!" I bounced in my chair.

"VIP tickets to see *Phantom* on Broadway? I don't care what people say, that guy is still hot even though his face is all messed up," she babbled. She leaned over in her chair to reach a bowl of cereal and started shoveling spoonfuls into her mouth.

"Even better!" I couldn't stop beaming now. *I am a genius.* "We're going to wish you home!"

Liv's hand froze in midair, her spoon dripping with milk. "What do you mean? Like wish that we never had to move here?" Her eyes darted around her room.

I blinked. "No, we can just wish for you to come home now! Isn't it great? Every other wish we've made has come true, so this is perfect! I think fate made you move when you did so we could use my half-birthday to undo it!" I leaned back and propped my feet up on the table. "Pretty great, right? It can be like you never left at all!"

And this is the part where she *should* have said, "Oh, Ana! This is the best idea you've ever had! Then I can come home and we can go back to being best friends who actually live in the same place again! What would I do without you?!"

But no.

Instead, she made a face. "What makes you think that will work?"

I rolled my eyes. "All our wishes have worked! Why would this be any different? We just both have to *believe*, like always," I explained. Honestly, how she was not jumping up and down at my idea was beyond me. This was my best idea since peanut butter and marshmallow sandwiches.

She resumed chewing again and shrugged. "I don't know. It seems like it might be a waste, you know?"

My heart sank. "A waste?! How would wishing for you to come back home be a waste? Don't you want to come back?" A dark feeling twisted around my chest.

She sighed. "It's not that," she said quietly. "It just seems like it would be a really hard wish to come true. And then when it didn't…"

"It *would*, though!" I interrupted. "You have to trust me. Tomorrow, at exactly eleven in the morning your time on my half-birthday, we have to make our wish. All you need to do is remember the rules, wear your lip gloss, and we'll do it together. And I promise, it will work." I nodded eagerly at the screen.

It has to.

I held my breath as Liv puckered her lips the way she always does when she's thinking something over. Part of me wanted to shake her. But the other part knew that deep down, she was probably just afraid we'd be disappointed. I couldn't blame her there.

"Okay," she said hesitantly. "We can try it."

I grinned. "Excellent! I'll find you here tomorrow right after school, okay? Get your cupcake ready!" I lifted my hand in triumph.

Liv nodded. "Armed with frosting!"

I clicked off the video chat and leaned back, letting a slow smile take over my face. The orangutan and "Save the Rain Forest" posters in the break room seemed to be cheering me on. By this time tomorrow, our wish would be made.

This was *so* going to work.

chapter 2

"Male peacocks use their huge, ornamented tail to attract female attention. Flashy male displays are a common way to successfully obtain a mate."

—*Animal Wisdom*

Mondays are a lot like lions hiding in the tall grass. They are always ready to pounce. And if you're going to school *without* your best friend, Mondays can be just as dangerous. Ever since Liv moved away, I felt like I was walking around with a giant target on my back. I had to pretend like nothing had changed.

But everything had changed.

I kept my head down as I walked to my locker before the bell rang. The halls of our school were buzzing with activity. Summer was almost here, and you could tell it was starting to get to everyone. Even the teachers would stare out the window, like they were looking at a giant slice of pie they wanted to scarf down.

Posters for the end-of-school dance (which they called the "School End Dance"—geniuses) were suspended from the ceilings and people were getting extra touchy-feely all over each other. What is it about upcoming dances and skirt weather that makes girls all eye-batty and guys more rowdy than usual? I mean, it's even on a Monday. Who has a dance on a *Monday*?

Middle school, that's who.

I shoved my backpack into my locker and dug around for a binder. Our final tests were coming up, and my May calendar stared me in the face on my locker door, with each test day marked with a sticker. My math test was the worst of all, looming on my calendar like a giant black hole instead of the cute little unicorn sticker Liv had given me. What if I didn't even pass? I could be stuck in the bottom end of junior high forever. All of the buildup made little flutters of anxiety buzz around in my stomach.

A palm tree sticker on my calendar reminded me about my English assignment. Mrs. Roca has this tradition where she makes us each stand up in front of the room and ramble on for exactly two minutes about a topic that she pulls from a hat. Seriously, she even has this moldy looking top hat specifically for these little torture sessions. We aren't allowed to say "um" or we lose points. My topic is Harry Houdini, and after coming up with a zillion excuses for the past month on why I wasn't ready, my big day was coming this week.

The only magical guy named Harry that I know anything about had a lightning bolt scar on his forehead, so there is no way I've got two minutes' worth. But mostly, the thought of standing at the front of the room while everybody secretly hopes for me to throw up like I did in fifth grade during group debates was almost enough to make me, well... throw up again. All those eyes just...staring at me.

"Um, can I get into here...?" A low voice interrupted my locker scan. A familiar knocking began in my chest. It was Zack. *The* Zack.

CREATURE FILE

SPECIES NAME: Zackardia Perfecticus

KINGDOM: Junior High

PHYLUM: Tennis Gods; Dimpled Carnivora (LOOK AT HIS DIMPLES!)—targeted crush of Sneerer Clan Apex: Ashley

WEIGHT: Just. Right.

NATURAL HABITAT: Unclear; species has never been seen outside of school habitat. Always has tennis ball in hand, so can probably be found at tennis courts.

FEEDS ON: Sports, video games, and Thursday ravioli at the caf.

LIFE SPAN: Not long enough.

HANDLING TECHNIQUE: I wish.

NOTE ZACKARDIA PERFECTICUS IS KNOWN TO APPEAR OUT OF NOWHERE. ENSURE PROPER HYGIENE AND HAIR CARE TO MINIMIZE EMBARRASSMENT FROM RANDOM ENCOUNTERS. ALSO, LIP GLOSS.

"Hey!" I cleared my throat. Did I just yell that? "Hey, Zack. Nice weather we're having, hmm?"

I actually said that. I wanted to tear out my vocal chords with a pen. I stepped aside so he could get into his locker, which was serendipitously placed beside mine.

I couldn't decide whether it was good or bad luck yet.

Given the last thirty seconds, bad.

Zack was the type of guy that should come with a warning label: Do not look at if you are operating heavy machinery, walking, or trying not to make a complete fool of yourself. Once, Liv caught me doodling a cartoon of Zack looking up at me on a balcony, Romeo and Juliet style. I even drew him holding flowers. *That's* how pathetically sad and insane it makes me having Zack pop up at a moment's notice.

Not only was he seriously the cutest guy in school, Zack was also a tennis star. Girls who couldn't even *spell* tennis showed up to his games. He also had the ability to make me stutter, a development I've noticed since the summer sun had given his hair a decidedly beachy look.

Mmm.

He slid a textbook into his locker with a thud, jerking me from my little daydream. Apparently if Zack is around, I have the attention span of a gnat. I stood there gaping at him, digging around in my head for the perfect, witty thing to say.

"Uh…" was all I came up with.

That's when I heard a high-pitched voice coming from down the hall. I wished for the hundredth time that I was invisible as I peeked past Zack.

The Sneerers.

Three girls swayed their hips as they walked in

their usual line formation. They each had on black skirts with a loose tank top clinging at their hips, each in a different color. I don't know how they managed it, but they always seemed to walk like there was a soundtrack playing for them—only they were the only ones who could hear it.

"Hey, Zack." Ashley gave a flirty wave as she approached us. I ducked my head behind my locker door, hoping they wouldn't notice me.

Ashley, Brooke, and Rayna were the worst part of my day. Every day. You know how some girls you're friends with earlier in school, say, first grade, but then something happens and they start hating on you for no reason?

Yeah. Ashley is nothing like that. We've never been friends. She's always hated me, and she *loves* to feel like she's super mature. She even wears a matching set of earrings and a necklace, which (as she told us a bazillion times) her mother got her when she got her first bra. Because of this (the attitude, the pearl earrings, and the solid B cup), I've always avoided her like a school-borne plague. Tweedledee and Tweedledum stick with her like those little scavenger fish around a shark, eager to get a bite of popularity from her. Actually, Ashley would make a pretty good shark because she's even on the swim team with Rayna. I can't imagine anyone that would *voluntarily* put on a Speedo under those nasty lights, but they seem to have some sort of supergene that makes their blond hair not turn green with all that chlorine. Brooke moved here a year or so ago, so she's currently the lowest rank on Team Sneerer.

CREATURE FILE

SPECIES NAME: Ashleydae Reignus

KINGDOM: Junior High

PHYLUM: Carnivora; Swim Team Goddesses

WEIGHT: I don't know, but they get full after two bites of sushi.

NATURAL HABITAT: The mall, but only the parts that are backlit with pink lighting.

FEEDS ON: The souls and pain of the weak, waterproof mascara, organic food, and *Teen Vogue*; also, my misfortune.

LIFE SPAN: Most witches and monsters in fairytales seek immortality, so...

HANDLING TECHNIQUE: AVOID AT ALL COSTS.

NOTE SPECIES RAYNAA PONTIFICUS AND BROOKENZI SNEEROFIDUS HAVE BEEN FOUND TO BE GENETIC CLONES OF SPECIES NOTED ABOVE.

"Hey, Scales." Ashley's voice dripped with sweetness. You could tell she was aware that Zack was listening by the way her eyes flitted to him every four seconds—such a shark. She swept a lock of blond hair from her eyes. The silver on her earrings twinkled in the light. "I hope there aren't any bugs in your pants today. Must be hard without Liv around to do your hair for you, huh?" She twirled her hair around her fingertip and eyed my ponytail with fake sympathy.

Seriously, ever since my idiot brother let slip that I was named after a snake—an anaconda to be precise—I hadn't heard the end of it. And the whole bug thing—so I accidentally left the house with a pocket full of crickets after feeding some of Daz's snakes. One time. Four years ago. If it hadn't been so mortifying, it would have been funny; they started chirping during Mr. Dixon's grammar lecture, and it sounded exactly like a movie where everybody gets bored. Usually the Sneerers had to face Liv whenever they made fun of me, but now? I am basically target practice.

"Hey, Ashley, did you know that some perfumes are made with whale vomit? Maybe you want to go a little easy on the spritzing tomorrow?"

I *so* wish I'd said that, but the voice belonged to someone else.

I swiveled around wide-eyed to see who had the guts to talk back to Ashley. A tall girl in red warm-up pants was half jogging toward us.

Rebecca!

I gulped and kept my eyes forward, not wanting to make eye contact. Rebecca was Ashley's older sister, and being in eighth grade, she was even more popular (and therefore scarier) than anyone our age in seventh. But she did it without being a kraken. Although it was sort of cool to see someone take a dig at Ashley. How could a nice girl like Rebecca be sisters with Ashley?

"Why don't you shut up, Becca?" Ashley spat at her sister.

Rebecca ignored her and smirked at me. My cheeks burned at the attention. "Ignore her. She's just miffed I beat her time at practice this morning, *again*. Aren't you, *kiddo*?" Rebecca reached out and punched Ashley playfully on the arm before sauntering away to her friends.

See? Some people seem to ooze confidence all over the place. Whereas the only thing I oozed was a bit of prickly sweat under my arms when I was nervous. Which was almost all the time.

I bit my tongue, unable to hide my smile. I guess sometimes the best way to deal with mean ones was to be mean right back? Of course, the thought of saying anything like that to Ashley made me want to lose my breakfast.

Ashley's perfectly stained lips pressed thin, and her face shifted to a grim mask of anger. She makes that face a lot, and it always makes me think her skin is going to melt off and reveal a metal robot skull and a flickering, short-circuited eyeball. I could see it.

She glared at me. "Whatever, geek. Smile all you want, but we'll see how happy you are in English class," she said, puffing up her chest. "I just talked to Mrs. Roca, and she said I could switch my talk with yours. So you'll be talking today, instead of the end of the week," she cooed. "She mentioned something about you putting it off long enough? *You're welcome*." Ashley's eyes were wide with phony innocence.

My stomach plummeted to the floor. I swear, the devil must take lessons from Ashley. Now what was I going to do?! Two minutes, two minutes… how could I avoid stage fright puking with such short notice?!

She turned on her heels and stomped away. Her

two minions followed but not before Rayna gave me the Look. The Look is the Sneerers' specialty, where they raise one eyebrow and make you (the target) feel as dumb/ugly/worthless as possible. They're really good at it. Sometimes it comes with a patented lip curl too.

As the Sneerers stormed off, Brooke nearly bulldozed straight into Bella, a tiny girl in our grade who always darted to class like a field mouse with her head stuck in a book. Her short, pixie-ish hair popped above the pages as Ashley yelled, "Walk much, Brooke?" Shoving her friend, she glared at Bella. "Look out, *freak*." She waved her hand dismissively, like she was swatting away flies instead of the awkward girl in front of her. Poor Bella.

I peeked up trying to give her a smile, but she bowed her head back into her book and flitted around the corner, away from the Sneerers.

"Woo! She's looking rather hot today, don't you think, Kev? How come you don't get yourself some nice clothes like that, Ana? Maybe you should spend more time primping and less time doodling in that notebook of yours," Daz said from behind me, poking at my shoulder.

CREATURE FILE

SPECIES NAME: Daz Ridiculosis

KINGDOM: Our house; third door on the left, with the skull and crossbones sign

PHYLUM: Idiot (large phylum, mainly comprised of spikey-haired reptile lovers)

WEIGHT: 120 pounds of sarcasm.

NATURAL HABITAT: Behind closed doors doing God-knows-what; at the pet shop terrorizing crickets; with Kevin, his male equivalent of a BFF.

FEEDS ON: Pizza, Kraft macaroni and cheese *with* ketchup (disgusting), music that is screamed rather than sung, anything with scales, scutes, or shells.

LIFE SPAN: Much too long.

HANDLING TECHNIQUE: Proceed with caution; Daz Ridiculosis can change temperament faster than a ticked-off Komodo.

I narrowed my eyes and spun to face him, gripping my notebook tight. So typical of Daz to be a turd and kick me when I'm down. I know I'm no

Picasso, but I don't make fun of him for all the geeko things he does.

Oh wait, I do.

"Nobody asked you!" I hissed. There ought to be a law against brothers attending the same school as their sisters.

Daz waggled an eyebrow with a crooked grin on his face. His best friend, Kevin, stood beside him, sketching something on a pad of yellow drafting paper. They were both wearing T-shirts and khaki shorts. Really, sometimes life seemed so much easier for guys. You didn't see anybody mocking their clothes, did you? And their hair? Don't even get me started—it's like they get extra points for having bedhead.

"What's with them?" Kevin asked, looking up to watch Ashley sway down the hall. Even though he was best friends with Daz, Kevin was totally different from Daz. Mainly in that I can tolerate him. And unlike my brother, who clearly had a look of appreciation in his eyes at Ashley's backside, Kevin seemed to watch her like she was some kind of science experiment.

CREATURE FILE

SPECIES NAME: Kevinidae Mechanogenius

KINGDOM: Any place Daz is; the robot club; computer lab

PHYLUM: Guys Who for Some Reason Think Daz Is Enjoyable Company and who Have Somewhat Nice Hair

WEIGHT: Undetermined.

NATURAL HABITAT: my kitchen (scarfing down Pizza Pops), the CERN lab (he wishes).

FEEDS ON: Pizza Pops (see above), an inordinate amount of citrus, his thumbnail.

LIFE SPAN: Despite über-nerd tendencies, he's managed to survive quite well this far. (Why is that? What's his secret?)

HANDLING TECHNIQUE: Will do anything for a gift certificate to the GameStop.

I shut my locker door and shook my head. "Welcome to the wonderful world of girls, Kev," I said, forcing my tight frown away. Liv would never let Ashley get away with being a jerk to me. She always had the best comebacks and never seemed to even care when the Sneerers snarked at us. Honestly, sometimes she even laughed. Without her, I felt like I was alone on a dinghy in a great big ocean of piranhas.

The anticipation of our wish buzzed inside me again. All I had to do was get through today.

"Oh," I said, yanking open my locker again. "You forgot your robot parts in my locker last week. Did you need them?" I pointed to the disembodied arms that littered the floor. Being a supersmart guy and all, Kevin was big into robots. They filled up his locker and even Daz's, so sometimes when he needed extra space, I let him use mine. I liked to think it would buy me karma points if the robots ever became self-aware and went after us all.

He frowned. "Sorry. I can pick them up tomorrow, once I clean mine up. Is that okay?" He gave me a sheepish look.

I shrugged. "No problem. Not like they can do much harm when they don't have bodies, right?" I snorted at my own joke and mentally cursed myself for being such a dweeb. But Kevin didn't seem to notice.

"Hey, Ana," he said, his eyes lighting up. "I can make it up to you! Daz said you're not doing so hot in math?"

I shot a glare at Daz, who simply shrugged.

"Ugh, *yes*," I muttered. "I mean, 'not so hot' is an understatement. I'm failing." The word tasted bitter in my mouth. "I don't know what an integer is and don't even get me started on common denominators."

I cringed as another wave of heat crawled over the back of my neck. I hated feeling stupid around Kevin.

"You want some help? I'm pretty good at math," Kevin said, chewing his thumbnail.

I scoffed. I was surprised "pretty good" was even in Kevin's vocabulary. "Nah, I'll be okay," I said. "I'll figure it out. Somehow. Thanks though." I gave him a smile, but it was hard to hide the panic that was lurking behind it. My life was crazy enough without inviting genius-boy Kevin in to inspect it.

Growing List of Things I Will Never Understand about Boys

1. How come none of them seem to *ever* worry about how they look? And yet, they all manage to look okay. Even Daz, a guy who spends exactly four minutes in the bathroom each morning and half of that is drawing on a fake mustache with Dad's shaving cream and chasing me around the hallway. But girls still look at him when he walks into a room, and *some* girls even think he's cute. Gross.

2. Kevin. Pretty much everything about him. The weird thing is, I used to think I understood *everything* about Kevin. He likes robots, and he's way too smart; he never drinks milk from

the carton, and he always checks with my mom before opening a new box of cereal or crackers. But lately? Something seems different about him. You know those kooky Magic Eye things that reveal a secret picture when you stare at them in just the right way? Kevin seems like that, only I have no idea what the secret picture is. And there's no way I'm going to stare at him to find out.

3. *Groups* of boys. When groups of girls get together, we mostly talk about school or boys or books, or pretty much anything else on the planet. But when BOYS get together, it seems like things get grosser and grosser. I heard Daz talking with a group of guys at school once and it was all boogers, farts, and scabs. If girls *only* saw guys in groups, nobody would have a crush on any of them, *ever*.

chapter 3

"Chameleons have special cells in their skin that can change color, depending on light, temperature, and their emotional mood."

—*Animal Wisdom*

If only I had special cells that could turn me invisible in English class, because I am SO not in the mood for this.

"And finally," I said, sneaking one last look at the sweaty notes on my palm, "Harry Houdini died when he was fifty-two, from a ruptured, um, appendix," I said. I stared at the back of the room, doing my best to ignore Ashley's snarky giggles from the sidelines.

Is there any better way to start an English class than by feeling like you're going to lose your

Froot Loops all over the first row? After the longest two minutes of my life, I scrambled back to my desk as Mrs. Roca, our English teacher, nodded. "Thank you, Ana. Next time, when you find yourself wanting to say 'um,' take a breath instead." She smiled at me.

Please. If I *knew* I was going to say "um" ahead of time, doesn't she think I would just, oh, I don't know, *NOT* say it? I was just happy it was over. I could still hear my heart banging away in my eardrums. There was nothing worse than being on display at the front of the room. What I didn't know was that Mrs. Roca's plan for the rest of class included the two worst words a student can hear: *assigned partners.*

She looked up over her glasses. "For the rest of the period, I'm going to partner you up so you can make your study list for your final exam. You can take today to catch up on any material you've missed, but starting tomorrow, your partner is your best friend here." She toyed with the thick African beads around her neck. Mrs. Roca is such a weirdo. She eats blue Jell-O every day at exactly 9:43 and *always* pronounces my name like "Ah-na," instead of plain old Ana, even though I've told her a bazillion times how to say it the right way.

My stomach began to knot. Liv was always my

partner, but she wasn't here. This was going to be terrible. For once, I wished Daz was in this class so I could at least partner with him. I searched the back of the room for Bella. Maybe we could partner? Mrs. Roca read off the partners, and we waited, ready for the executioner's ax.

"Ms. Wright," she finally said. "You will partner with Ms. Evans." She pointed to the stone-cold face that was eyeing me from the side of the room.

Brooke. Ashley's third in command. Also known as Orange-You-Glad-I-Self-Tanned Evans. She glared at me warily, and then very slowly began to shake her head back and forth. I felt a thousand imaginary spiders crawling all over me. I was toast.

Ashley made a disgusted sound behind her but clammed up fast when Mrs. Roca paired her with Mark, one of Zack's best friends.

Honestly, sometimes I think teachers are mean for the sake of being mean.

"What crawled into your cave and died, Scales? You look more disheveled than normal." Brooke settled in across from my desk a few minutes later, with her arms crossed over her chest. I knew she didn't mean it as anything but an insult, but the fact that Brooke noticed how terrible I looked stung pretty hard. Normally she doesn't notice anybody that isn't...her.

33

I wiped my eyes and looked longingly at the back of the room where Bella was partnered with Rachel, a girl who played field hockey. They looked like they were having fun.

Just get through today, I told myself again. *After your wish today, you and Liv will be partners for every project again.* I glanced at the clock on the wall. Only a couple hours left!

"Okay, what other essay questions do you think we should be worried about here?" I ignored Brooke's comment and flipped to a fresh page in my notebook, skimming past my version of Mrs. Roca being chased by a walrus in the margins. She glared at me for a moment, popped a giant bubble of bright pink gum, and returned to look at her nails.

Clearly asking her what she thought was the wrong way to approach this.

"I'm thinking we should probably make sure we know about *To Kill a Mockingbird*," I said, shaking my head at the fact that I was even trying. "Mrs. Roca spent a lot of time on that one, and with it being a classic and all…" I looked up to her for her reaction.

Pop!

"Whatever you say." Her heavily mascaraed lashes dropped back down to her notebook, which was covered in notes from her and Ashley. I could also make out a bunch of cartoon flowers, with their wilted petals falling toward the bottom of the page. They were pretty good, actually.

Guess I wasn't the only doodler in the room.

"I'm not happy about this either," I said. "I know you'd much rather be working with Ashley." I lowered my voice, so I didn't catch her attention. "But we really need to do this. The exam is in less than two weeks. You want to pass, don't you?"

She raised one eyebrow into a cold arch, but the rest of her face stayed the same. I'd have to practice that move in the mirror, because it gave me chills. Her brown eyes slid behind me toward Ashley, who was too busy adjusting her boobs for maximum cleavageness to notice.

"I think *Mockingbird* will definitely be on the exam," she said softly, but kept the hard look in her eyes.

I tried to hide my shock by clearing my throat. Was there a glitch in the matrix or something? Or had Brooke actually spoken to me without hurling an insult?

Weird.

I blinked, then flipped back in my notebook to our study notes from the start of the year. "She asked us to write about why the author would choose a young narrator…but she didn't have that on the last test…" I looked up.

"Is that supposed to be Ashley?" she piped up, grabbing my notebook before I could stop her. She flipped it over and inspected a sketch from my last class, her eyes narrowed.

I was so dead meat. Why had I drawn Ashley as a dragon?! This was actual evidence that could be used against me. Mayday!

"Ah," I said, clearing my throat. "No, of course not." I tried to keep the fear from my eyes. Sneerers can smell fear a mile away, like a shark smelling a drop of blood in the water.

I winced as she tilted the notebook on its side, getting a closer look. "You've got her eyes right," she said, biting her lip. "The tail is too long, I think. Maybe give her claws too," she added, handing it back to me with a sly smile.

Uhh…

Brooke began scribbling notes with her lime-green pen. "Anyway, yeah. *Mockingbird.* That sounds about right." She paused for a minute, underlining some words on her page. "I really need to pass this exam," she breathed quietly, more to herself than me. Her shoulders slumped over her desk.

I looked up from my page. "Not doing so hot?" It felt oddly nice to think that one of the Sneerers was failing something in life, even if it was only English.

I tried not to show relief on my face as I flipped my incriminating sketch behind some pages.

She grimaced, scrunching up her dainty nose. "Yeah, I didn't pass the last test." She reached down into her bag and pulled out a small pocket nail file in the shape of a sunflower. "Too many books on our list. And Ashley wanted us to fund-raise for the swim team, so I haven't had time," she mumbled. "Posters and stuff," she said when I gave her a quizzical look. She began filing her nails, with her mouth pulled into a tight thin line.

"Oh. That…sucks. Yeah, I think Mrs. Roca must think we're all speed-reading robots," I said absently, watching the quick, deliberate movements of the sunflower as she filed.

"Why do you do it?" I blurted. I lowered my voice to a whisper. "I mean, you're not even on the swim team. So why do you get stuck making posters?" I don't know why I asked. I had a feeling I already knew the answer.

Her glance darted to Ashley. "She's dead set on raising the most money this year," she said, shrugging. She stared down at her hands. "Her sister is, like, hard-core competitive." She leaned closer to me. "Rebecca wins the fund-raiser prize *every* year." She nodded secretively to me, like this should explain everything.

"Huh," I said. I'd never met this Brooke before. She seemed a lot smaller than usual. Deep inside, it made me sort of happy that Ashley didn't feel good enough compared to her sister. But really, her sister was so much *nicer*, it seemed almost fair. Having a sister had to be better than a brother, I bet. Even if she was mean or competitive.

"Hey," I said, peering over at her fingers. Tiny flowers were painted on near her cuticles. "I really like your nail polish. You're good at that." My throat felt tight giving her a compliment.

She smiled broadly, then looked back through her dark bangs to see if Ashley was watching. "Thanks. Whenever I get nervous, I file them. Or paint them. It sort of helps me"—she considered for a moment—"focus."

She flicked the file across her nail once more and held her hand out to inspect it. "Probably doesn't help much." She shrugged, straightening up. "So. What else do you think we should study?"

The next forty-five minutes with Brooke belonged in some fantasy novel, because they sure as heck didn't seem real. Although she never once really looked at me—or heaven forbid, cracked another smile—she actually helped make real study notes. She even said that I could get rid of the bags under my eyes with some cotton balls soaked in coffee. True, that's sort of an insult wrapped in a snarky instructional, but it's something.

Strange Things about Girls That I Will Never Understand, Despite Being One

1. How come some girls seem to intuitively know how to do their hair perfectly? Like Brooke, for example. She's the only brunette in the Sneerers (which I think Ashley holds against her), but she always knows how to do her hair in those messy-but-perfect updos. If I tried that, I'd look like a microwaved scarecrow. Where do they learn this stuff? I barely have the ability to brush my teeth without stabbing myself in the face. Is there an online forum that can help me? YouTube?

2. Likewise, the muffin top. Why can't all girls have it, so we can level out the playing field? Not that I would wear thong underwear and have bright pink straps hanging out from my jeans like Ashley does, but a definitive lack-of-muffin-top would make things a lot easier. There must be a compromise here.

3. Personalities. Sometimes I think that girls have two (or more) of them. Brooke around Ashley is worse than a moody hyena, but without Ashley

she becomes almost…nice. Interesting even. But Ashley always seems the same: nasty as a badger. And from what I can tell, the only thing worse than being enemies with her is being *friends* with her. How do girls keep track of all this? And how can I make sure that Evil Brooke does not randomly show up while we're knee-deep in study notes in English?

The bell at the end of the day couldn't ring soon enough. When it finally did, I made a mad dash for my locker, gathered my things, and powerwalked home before the buses were even pulling out of the parking lot. I didn't care that you look like a dweeb when you powerwalk, with your elbows stuck out like you're wearing swim floaties. I didn't care that I was probably forgetting some homework under the robot mess in the bottom of my locker. And I really didn't care that I almost slipped in a pile of dog you-know-what on the sidewalk in my race home.

All that mattered was that it was wish time.

Having Liv home again would make all that stuff not matter.

I bolted into the kitchen and rummaged around in the cabinet, searching for the package of chocolate cupcakes that I'd hidden from Daz, tucked behind the microwave. I clutched the package in my hand as I ran upstairs to my bedroom, sighing with relief when I saw the clock.

Perfect timing.

I unwrapped the crinkly foil and set the cupcake in front of me, ready to go. Already the relief was making me giddy.

"This is going to work, Darwin!" I giggled at the shiny yellow eyes staring up at me and poked my finger through the metal bars of his cage. Charles Darwin is my African gray parrot, but I only call him his full name when he poops on my head and he's in trouble. This happens more than I'd like to admit. We even have a teeny picture of the *real* Charles Darwin, all bearded and serious looking, stuck to his cage in case bird-Darwin is ever curious about his namesake.

Darwin's super smart and has been my friend for years, ever since Mom brought him home from a veterinarian she works with at the zoo. He can't fly because of a wonky wing, but he sure can talk. I like to think he's pretty happy here with us because I spoil him rotten with fruit and veggie treats. I also bring him up to my room *every* night so he doesn't have to sleep in the empty living room by himself. It's fun, even though sometimes it's like having a feathery toddler over for a sleepover. Ooh! Liv and I could have summer sleepovers soon too!

Clicking my laptop, I found Liv's name and waited for her to answer. The smell of chocolate wafted to my nose, making my stomach growl.

Riiiinnnnnngggg!

I edged closer to my screen. I wonder what kind of cupcake Liv would have? Cupcakes must be easy to find there, right? Maybe they had weird New Zealandy flavors? I uncapped my lip gloss and slicked some on.

Riiinnnnnnngggg!

Grinning to myself, I imagined what life would be like once she was back home. We would have a whole summer to hang out. The last summer before eighth grade. It would be *epic*. Now where *was* she?

Riiinnnnnnngggg!

A white bubble popped up on my screen.

> **We're sorry. This user is not answering. Try again later?**

My jaw dropped. There had to be some sort of mistake. I clicked exit and started the program again. Glitches happen all the time. I ignored the menacing feeling in my gut. So long as we made our wish at the same time together, it would still be okay. There was plenty of my half-birthday left.

But Liv didn't answer the time after that.

Or the time after that.

Tears began to fill my eyes as I stared at my cupcake.

"Hello?" I said to no one. The walls around me felt like they were squishing in closer and closer.

"Talking to yourself, weirdo?" Daz popped into my room.

I wiped my eyes hastily. "Get out of here! I'm talking to Liv!" I lowered my laptop screen, but kept it open just in case she showed up. It had been twenty minutes now. This didn't make any sense. Liv is one of those people who shows up early to *everything*.

Daz nodded. "Liv looks a lot different than I remember her. Much hairier." He gestured to my desktop background, with one of Mom's photos of her lions staring back at us. "Ooh, cupcakes," he said, snatching the one in the wrapper. He offered a piece to the snake around his neck before wolfing it down.

"Who said that was for you?" I exclaimed. "Why are you even here?" I looked sadly at the screen again. Still no Liv.

Daz opened his eyes wide and did his best to look innocent. Which, given that he is my brother, is totally unbelievable and phony. Daz could be comatose and he still wouldn't be innocent.

He held up his hands. "Hey, I just got home and heard you babbling to yourself," he said. "I figured

I'd make sure you hadn't lost your marbles." He licked his lips, sending crumbs dropping to his shirt and bouncing off the snake's pink-striped body.

"It's my half-birthday," I said halfheartedly. The tears were coming back again, but I did my best to not blink them out. "We were…we were supposed to wish." I pointed feebly to the screen. *Why* had she not shown up? It was becoming too real now. The disappointment felt like a heavy, smothering blanket over me.

He perked up. "It's your half-birthday? If it's your half-birthday, that means it's also *my* half-birthday. Happy half-birthday to us!" He grabbed the other cupcake in front of me and gulped it down in one disgusting bite. "Hey, don't forget Mom said it's our turn to do dishes tonight. Not it!" He bounded out into the hall before I could respond.

I glared at my laptop. You'd think that being twins, we'd have *something* in common. But Daz is *such* an alien. What do you expect from someone named Daz? If he were at Hogwarts, he'd totally be a Slytherin, while I'd be stuck in Hufflepuff or the other one that nobody remembers.

"Whatever," I huffed. I opened up a new tab to start an e-mail.

Dear Liv.

No. That didn't sound nearly serious enough. Why wasn't she here right now so we could wish her home already?! I deleted the line and started again.

HEY. It's after school and I'm wondering where you are. I thought we had our cupcake wish planned? Are you okay? If you get this in time, find me tonight and we can still make our wish!

I hit the send button hard.

"BRAACK! WHATEVER!" Darwin squawked. His feathers bristled as he shook his wings out.

Hello, my name is Ana, and I am completely, totally, and most definitely alone.

chapter 4

"Cheetahs are the only cats that can't
retract their claws."

—*Animal Wisdom*

I wish I had claws. And not the fake kind from
the drugstore either. But real ones. Then I
could threaten Daz and anyone else who tries
to ruin my day.

When it was finally time for dinner that night, I
felt like a flea on a grizzly. Completely small and
overwhelmed. I still hadn't heard from Liv, and no
matter how hard I tried, I couldn't figure out what
could be so important to keep her from our wish.
Didn't she want to come home?

"Look, Ana! *Look!*"

I stopped doodling a picture of a moldy cupcake and looked at Daz across the table. He had a pair of ancient iPod earbuds up his nose.

"Now watch!" He hit play on the device and opened his mouth wide. Music began to play, the loud riffs of some angry punk band pumping out of his mouth like it was a radio.

"Your mouth becomes a speaker! How cool is that?" His eyes shone with excitement as I glared at his open mouth. Sometimes, it was like he was four years younger instead of four minutes. There should be an exchange policy on brothers.

"Hello, you two." Mom sauntered in and sat at the table. She looked quizzically at Daz, who had stuck the buds back into his nose and was opening and closing his mouth like a guppy. She blinked and shook her head. She should—*she* made him.

As usual, Mom was decked out in her safari gear. Don't get me wrong, she's actually seriously pretty with dirty blond hair and gray eyes. And even though she's old, like forty, she only looks about thirty-five or so. At least she does when her hair is washed and not covered in some ridiculous safari hat. But, because of their work, both she and Dad look sort of weird. Picture an African safari guide, only with a zoo badge and handheld radios. My dad even has to carry a gun some days!

So what if it's a tranquilizer gun? Nobody has to know that.

"What were your highs and lows today?" She looked at each of us with bright eyes.

Daz spoke first. "My high was finding the lost treasure of Atlantis." He grinned, ignoring Mom's skeptical eyebrow. "And my low was losing it down a sewer. Now the world will never know, Mother. It will never know…" He shook his head mournfully.

What a clown.

"And you?" She turned to me.

I swallowed thickly. "My low was having a special video chat with Liv, and…" I could barely say the words. "And she missed it."

Mom's face softened. "That's too bad, hun. I'm sure she didn't mean it, and she's got to be busy with the move. She'll probably call you tomorrow," she said, getting up to stir the bubbling pot of pasta sauce.

Yeah. Too bad tomorrow would be too late for our awesome wish. I swear, if there were a place called Bright Side, my mother would be queen. Complete with a little crown of stars and glitter and happy unicorns of opportunity.

"Hey, gang," Dad said, shuffling into the kitchen. He threw his hat on the back of his chair and doled out our plates, followed by a handful of mismatched cutlery. That's when the blast of a musical car horn made me practically jump out of my skin.

"What the heck?" Daz said, scurrying from his chair to look out the front window. "Mom! Mom, come look!" he yelled, yanking back the curtains. Electric blue and red lights flashed through the window, sending streams of color along the wall.

"Is that the police? Henry, go see what's going on," Mom said, looking stricken. Dad shoved his chair out from the table and headed for the front door.

"No!" Daz yelled from the living room. "I think it's…"

I pushed him out of the way, trying to get a better look. A giant, Caribbean-blue RV trailer was parked outside our house, with steel drum music pumping through the speakers mounted on top. The words "Shep Foster's Wild Across America Tour" were plastered to the side of the RV in hot pink lettering.

"It can't be," I whispered. Fear choked my throat, and I had to clutch the curtain to stay upright. No, no, no, no, please, a million times no to this.

Just then, the smoke alarm in the kitchen went off.

"Jane!" Dad yelled from the door. "It's Shep! It's your father! And some woman!"

Daz took another look out the window and gasped, then raced up to his room.

"Daz, where are you going? Get back down here

and see your grandfather!" Now it was Mom's turn to yell. She grabbed my hand and thrust me out the front door. I winced at the blasting music. The whole street was looking now, with neighbors peeking out from behind their curtains. "Go say hi and help them in," she hissed. "I've got to deal with that darn smoke alarm." She bustled back to the kitchen.

At that moment, I would have rather been in that burning pot of noodles than standing on the porch.

Ugh. I suppose I should mention that my grandfather is pretty much a celebrity. He's a naturalist, sort of like my mom and dad, but instead of working at a zoo, he travels all over making movies and documentaries about animals. Sometimes he does really crazy stuff, like swim with great whites without a cage and sleep in rattlesnake-infested deserts.

For *fun*.

He once filmed a reality television series about how long he could live in the jungle with his latest girlfriend without either of them succumbing to malaria or death by leaf-cutter ants. *TV Guide* gave it a great review. Top that off with the fact that he's had more dates than Prince Harry, and you've got yourself an A-list grandpa. The last I heard he was dating some actress from Hollywood or something. At least that's what the tabloid said. I just knew I was lucky that nobody at school had figured out I was related to him, since we have Dad's last name instead of his.

He got to me before I could run. Maybe it was the years of working with venomous snakes and snapping crocodiles, but my grandpa is always pretty quick on his feet. He was on the porch before I could say anything and swept me up in a hug, squashing me with his strong arms.

"My Ana banana. It is so good to see you!" He held me back by the shoulders to get a better look at my face. His deep tan was set off by the bright flowers and dolphins on his shirt. "You've gotten so *tall*. Must take after her mother, huh? Ha ha! Sugar! Take a look at my gorgeous granddaughter!" His laugh echoed under our porch ceiling and out through the street. He grabbed me by the cheeks and planted a big kiss on my forehead. The smell of woodsy cologne wafted around me. But Grandpa wasn't alone.

I tried to stop my eyes from bugging out at the blond woman who tottered up our driveway in bright red stilettos. She looked about seven feet tall, six of which were just her legs. Her miniskirt was deep blue and sequined, and she wore a black lace tank top over her (how do I put this?) *ample* chest. She looked like a mermaid from Las Vegas.

"She *is* gorgeous!" she trilled, appraising my

T-shirt and cutoffs as she clicked up the stairs. (Clearly this woman was a liar.)

She paused for a moment to reach down and pull a chunk of grass from her heel and beamed her dazzling white teeth at me. "It's fab to meet you, Ana. Shep never stops talkin' about y'all." She sounded like a character from those western movies Dad likes. Her head shook like a bobblehead so fast that I was afraid she'd lose the large diamond studs in her earlobes.

I stared at her, desperately wishing that the neighbors would stop watching. Fat chance of that.

"Hi. Thanks," I said, grasping blindly behind me for the doorknob. "You guys should come inside. You must be"—I eyed Leggy McSequins timidly—"hungry?"

She looked like she'd be full after one M&M.

"Oh, yes," my grandpa said. "You guys go ahead, and I'll give the camera crew directions to the hotel. Plenty of time for all that soon enough—I want to catch up with my family!" He slapped me on the back and hopped down to the lawn toward the RV, leaving Leggy staring at me.

I desperately wanted to shove her inside before we attracted any more attention. Some neighbors had stepped out onto their porches now, watching the chaos unfold.

"I'm sorry, but he called you 'Sugar'—I don't know your actual name," I said, slamming the door behind us and pulling the thin curtain over the window. Dad followed behind us.

She giggled and plopped her tiny green handbag onto the small table by the front door. "It *is* Sugar, silly. Sweet as candy, 'cept I won't give you a cavity!" She nudged me with her shoulder.

Good Lord.

I gritted my teeth and swiveled around to check for Mom.

There was a loud crash and then Mom emerged from the kitchen with a towel on her shoulder and a waft of thick smoke billowing out around her. She tripped as she noticed Sugar, who lit up like a Christmas tree.

"You must be Jane!" Sugar cooed, rushing over to grip Mom in a tight hug. Mom stood rigidly and patted her on the back awkwardly, a messy spoon in her hand.

"Let's take this party to the dining room," Dad said, nudging for me to grab some extra plates and cutlery. "Never a dull moment when your grandfather arrives," he said dryly, giving me a wink.

"Great idea, Henry. Sugar, you and Dad are welcome to join us for dinner," she said, tidying her messy hair. "Daz!" she called out, eyeing the stairs angrily. "Get *down* here and say hello to your grandpa and his...girlfriend." She ushered us all into the dining room with a look of determination in her eyes. It was the same look she wore when she had to deal with angry lions.

A few minutes later, I helped Mom scoop spaghetti and sauce onto our plates and listened while Grandpa started up with the adventure stories from his tour.

"I'm not kidding, Henry—he was forty-two feet long! Right there in the middle of the river! The whole village was lucky not to have been eaten by the dang thing!"

Sugar was beside me, nodding gravely at the thought of a forty-two-foot-long snake.

Right when my mom was about to yell for him again, Daz sauntered in. And boy, did he look like a moron.

His usual wacky hair had been gelled down, leaving only a flip of hair above his forehead spiking forward. He had also replaced his death metal T-shirt with a blue-and-white-striped button-up that he only wears on the rare occasion Mom drags us to a fancy gala for the zoo. I caught his eye and shook my head in disappointment.

My own brother, gone to the dark side.

"Hey, Grandpa," he said casually, sliding into

his seat and straightening out his plate. He nodded at Grandpa, then turned to Sugar, who was sitting beside me, checking her teeth in a spoon.

"And you must be?" He gave her a crooked smile and shoved his arm in front of my face to reach hers. He sounded weird to me, then I realized it was probably because he was lowering his voice a couple of octaves, so he sounded like a croaky frog. I doubted he could keep it up.

Mom cleared her throat and looked at my dad, who did nothing but pile some spaghetti onto his plate. "This is Sugar, Daz," she said, giving his new hair the "are-you-an-idiot?" look.

Sugar giggled and reached out to clasp Daz's hand, but instead of keeping her thumb up like a normal person, it was more of a dainty finger-drape sort of handshake.

"I beg your pardon, young man?" Grandpa sputtered. "You don't see me for years and now all of a sudden you're 'Hey, Grandpa-ing' me? I don't think so!" Grandpa shoved out of his chair, and to Daz's horror, snatched him right up from his chair into a totally nonmanly hug. He ruffled his hair under his fist and laughed. "That's much better. Good to see you, son." He let Daz go and chuckled at the state of his hair. Now he looked like he'd been electrocuted.

That'll teach him.

"DAZ IS A PAIN!" Darwin nattered, shimmying on his perch as he watched us eat. I choked on a mouthful of spaghetti, trying not to laugh. I'd taught him that little gem in less than a week.

Grandpa swiveled to look at him, nodding with appreciation. "I like this bird." He gestured to Darwin with his thumb. Darwin clicked his beak happily at him.

"So how did you and Sugar meet?" Daz asked, which caused Sugar to perk up with another dazzling smile.

"It's such a darling story, isn't it, dear?" She batted her eyes at Grandpa. I glanced at Mom, who looked as grossed out as I felt.

"I was in Hollywood for an audition," she said.

An actress. Surprise!

Daz piped in, "You're an actress! That's great. I bet you'll be super famous one day." He nodded wildly and practically frothed at the mouth.

Sugar touched her chest and bowed her head at him with a little giggle. "So, the audition went fine"—she leaned to my mom like she had a secret and said—"although I never did get it. They gave the part to some *floozy*." She waved at the air with a manicured nail. "Anyways! What was I saying? Right! Well, who would believe it, but I broke one of my heels on the pavement on the way out!"

Daz looked shocked. "Oh no…that's terrible!"

I shot him a look as Sugar continued. He was such a dolt.

"And your grandpa saw me, hobbling along outside the studio, looking as disheveled as a popsicle in July…"

Dad raised his eyebrows at Mom.

"And he just appeared out of nowhere and scooped me up in his arms! Said he couldn't bear to see such a pretty girl hobbling along the street with one shoe on!" She turned to him with glassy eyes. "Shep's so thoughtful." She grinned at him and reached out to touch his cheek, a rock the size of a small planet perched on her middle finger.

Oh, please. Grandpa randomly picks her up, *literally*, without even knowing her? I'd have called the cops if some guy tried that.

Grandpa grinned at her, then looked back at Mom. Her jaw was clenched, and she was blinking so fast I was sure I'd see smoke. Daz, on the other hand, was so enthralled with Sugar's story that he didn't even notice his mouth had been hanging open the entire time. I kicked him under the table, but he just spit quietly on his palms and ran them through his hair again.

Has there ever been a grosser dinner?

Just as the tension was starting to rise again and

my mom had lifted her finger to point at Grandpa and say something, Dad spoke up.

"So," he said. "To what do we owe the big surprise? *Really*, if you'd have called, we could have made something nicer." He eyed Sugar, while handing her a basket of garlic bread.

I twirled my pasta, trying to ignore the clenching feeling inside my stomach, while Daz gawped over Sugar cutting her noodles into tiny pieces. There was a napkin tucked into her tank top as a makeshift bib, and I'm pretty sure that if it hadn't been there, Daz would have been covered in drool.

Grandpa beamed. "Well, if you'd read the latest issue of *Entertainment Network*, you might have seen a little interview with yours truly! Maybe my beautiful granddaughter should announce the news." He reached into his pocket and pulled out ripped page from a glossy magazine and handed it to me. I blinked at the headline and read it aloud with a wavering voice.

Reality Star and Naturalist Plans Documentary

In entertainment news, fans will be delighted to hear that Shep Foster is planning a documentary of his life, with friends and family slotted to make guest appearances. The sixty-three-year-old reality star and naturalist, known for his rugged charm, outgoing personality, and trademark Hawaiian shirts, has been touring the world recently, promoting his new book, Wild Thing. *With both his daughter and son-in-law working at a zoo, Shep said he was eager to take some well-deserved time off to visit them, begin the documentary, and provide some funding for his daughter's project that will focus on large carnivores. "I can't wait to visit," Shep told us. "I haven't seen my grandkids in ages! It's been great to travel, but I'm looking forward to seeing them most of all."*

I set the paper down. "What does that mean? Guest appearances—what does that *mean*?" The spaghetti was twisting up in knots inside my stomach. "Mom?" I asked.

But she was too busy staring in awe at her dad.

"You're...you're funding my carnivore project?" Her eyes were misty. Grandpa reached over to touch her hand. "Of course I am, Janie," he said. "It's about time those bozos at the zoo knew what they have in you!"

Mom stammered, wiping her mouth with a napkin. "Dad, that's amazing. Thank you!" She looked at Dad, all googly-eyed.

"Wait, is this that lion project thing you wanted

to do?" I asked. I gripped my fork hard. Daz peered at her curiously and slurped a noodle.

"Yes! The one with the place inside!" She gripped her hands into fists and shook them in the air.

The place inside.

Three little words. But they latched on to my chest and pressed down until I could barely breathe.

I knew what she meant. The zoo had a few houses on the grounds, mostly for staff that had to be there around the clock for feeding or veterinary help. The houses were tucked in the back, in between the exhibits. Normally you walk right by them without noticing, mainly because they look like huts or fake base camps and are plastered with "Save Our Tigers" posters.

"But that means," I started. I couldn't finish that sentence without throwing up.

"We're gonna be living in the *zoo!*" Daz shrieked. He slammed down his fork and high-fived Sugar, who was giggling with delight.

All of my energy drained down through my toes and out my chair when I saw how happy they were. This couldn't be happening. First Liv moves away and now I'm expected to live in a *zoo*? Like a real zoo, with monkeys and lions and crocodiles as my neighbors? Without Liv, I wanted to stay anonymous. How the heck can I do that if I live in a zoo? Why did I have to be in the weirdest family on the planet?

"It will only be for a few months," Mom added. "A summer thing, really. You'll have so much fun!"

Gag me with a spoon. Not everyone is cool enough to be in the spotlight like Grandpa and Mom. *Some* people get called "Scales" every second of the day, no matter how much they try to pull off the whole "cool and confident" shtick.

"And this documentary you're filming—is it true that you would like us to be featured in it?" Dad asked. "How big are we talking here? Both of the kids are finishing up school, and I know that their exams are soon…"

I glanced at the newspaper article beside me. It practically glared back at me.

Grandpa put down his fork so he didn't poke himself in the eye; he was such a hand talker. "Well, the producers said they'd like to feature my family if they could. They already got a lot of footage of ol' Sugar here." He patted her on the shoulder.

"Oh, I'll bet they have," Mom said quietly, as she twirled her fork.

Grandpa ignored her. "And I've got a few public appearances now that I'm here. The bookstore in the Downsview Mall wants to have a signing for *Wild Thing*, and a few of the TV news stations around here have already talked to Herb for an interview with you all. I'd like to focus the footage on you guys, of course."

Honestly, at that point I stopped being able to feel my face. The half smile that I had plastered to my face sort of froze, and I was left with what I can only imagine was a zombielike sneer. I looked at my parents in horror.

I have to be on TV.

My stomach lurched. I felt the distinct tremor of sickness in my throat. Everything from the past week was all balled together, making my hands sweat and tremble.

I am going to puke.

Instead of arguing for my chance at freedom from insanity, my last chance to cling to anonymity, I, Ana Wright, shoved my chair out from the table and dashed upstairs to the bathroom, where I got a front row seat to the second viewing of my dinner.

Take that, Hollywood.

chapter 5

"Elephants can communicate with sounds
well below the human hearing range."
                                        —*Animal Wisdom*

This just in: I have to communicate with my
best friend over the Internet from now on,
because she can't be bothered to show up for
a cupcake wish.

When I sat down at my bench in art class the next
day, the smell of paint and clay felt like a warm hug
from a friend. All I wanted to do was lay low and
make it to summer, so Daz had promised not to
tell anyone at school about Grandpa. Okay, he had
bartered dish duty for a month, but it was worth it
to avoid the Sneerers finding out. The only thing

worse than them knowing I'm a scaredy-cat zoo freak would be them knowing I'm related to people who are *so* much cooler and braver than me.

Hello, I don't need that comparison.

All of this might not be nearly so bad if Liv was here. Before she moved, she used to glue tiny googly eyes on my binder whenever I was upset about something. But now? She's got better things to do, and it feels like I'll never have my best friend back again. How do I know this? Because last night, my life got so much worse.

Embarrassing grandfather shoving me into a TV interview? Check.

Parents forcing us to move into a zoo? Check.

Best friend ditching me for the rest of our lives? CHECK, CHECK, AND CHECK.

That's right.

You'd think that Liv would have had to have been in some awful accident to miss our cupcake wish, right? You'd think she would want to come back home so we could be best friends together again and do all the things that best friends should, like marry brothers and buy nice purses in matching colors.

But you'd be wrong.

When I clicked open my e-mail late last night, *this* is what I saw.

Dear Ana,

Sorry I missed our cupcake wish. I know it was impor-tant to you, and I feel super bad about bailing. The thing is, I sorta like it here, you know? I mean, it's not HOME yet, but it's crazy beautiful, and the people are really nice, and I just don't know if that's the right wish to make. I've never gotten to explore someplace cool and new before, and this whole adventure is kind of fun! I even met a girl with purple hair! Her name is Leilani, and she plays the flute. I know, I can see your face now all scrunched up and mad at me. I really am sorry. I know we can still be best friends from where we are too!

Love and milkshakes (the strawberry kind),

Liviola XOXO

Can you believe it?

I must have stared at all those exclamation marks for an hour, wondering how they had the nerve to look so happy and upbeat in such an awful e-mail.

It didn't matter what I did. Liv was *gone*. Officially, one hundred percent, not coming back *gone*, and I knew it. No wishing would fix that now. How could something be so true yet still feel so wrong? All day long, I kept picturing her millions of miles away, acting completely happy to be without *her* best friend. Why couldn't I do the same?

I yanked myself back to reality and forced myself to sit taller. I just had to make it through the rest of the school year. Ms. Fenton's familiar writing was scrawled out on the chalkboard, spelling out *My Seventh-Grade True Self* in loopy cursive. She had surrounded it with blue and green stars. A small ray of hope blossomed in my chest to see her cheerful writing.

Apart from sleep-in Saturdays and ice-cream sundaes, art class was one of my favorite things in the world. On our first day at the beginning of the year, Ms. Fenton had given us all a fabric-covered notebook, saying it could be for words or doodles, or even recipes or a stamp collection. *Anything*, she'd said, *that gets your creative self buzzing*. I'd always liked doodling, especially animals from the zoo, but it wasn't until meeting Ms. Fenton that I realized some people made art for a *living*. I couldn't picture myself doing that, but I loved the feel of having a pencil in my hand and the scritchy-scratch sound as I doodled on the paper. I filled up that first notebook in just three weeks, and she'd kept on giving me fresh ones every time I needed one.

My bench was closest to the window, so I was

staring out at the waving trees when Ms. Fenton finally appeared in the room. I know some art teachers are pretty loopy, but Ms. Fenton was pretty put together. She has a short crop of auburn hair that curls under her ears like a model, and long fingers that always look so elegant when she draws something for us on the board. She even has a glittery ring on her thumb that she got from France. France! I can *so* picture her in that big art gallery with a baguette in her backpack.

"Listen up, my little rutabagas!" She shuffled to the front of the room with an armful of paints. Plunking them down on the bench in front of her, she hopped up onto her desk and crossed her legs. That was how cool Ms. Fenton was—she didn't sit *at* her desk; she sat on it.

"The school year is almost up, and your hormones are probably turning you all into little monsters," she said, giving the class a wink and everyone laughed. "To help ease your transition into summer, I've decided to go easy on you…"

The class erupted into a cheer, which she encouraged with a little desk-dance of her own.

"By giving you one last project."

Cue the moaning.

"Don't worry. You'll love it," she reassured us.

"How about we do a project on naps?" Mark

shouted, fake snoring loudly. Some teachers would get upset at outbursts like that, but in Ms. Fenton's class, everyone seemed to be a little nicer, a little happier. She shook her head.

"Maybe next year, Mark," she said, tossing a piece of her chalk at his bench. He caught it and began doodling on the corner.

"As you can see from the board, your last project is going to be called 'My Seventh-Grade True Self.'" The class quieted as she spoke. "All I want you to do, using whatever medium you choose, is to show me who you are *today*, to commemorate your time here in seventh grade."

A hand shot up.

"Dan?"

"Can we use clay?" Dan asked, shoving his glasses farther up on his nose.

She nodded. "Any medium at all. Paints, clay, pastels, collage, colored pencils, anything! So long as you're using your hands to make it, and we have a teeny chat, explaining your choices. I'm hoping to have some of them displayed during the summer, so new seventh-grade students *next* year can see your work, as inspiration."

A few buzzes of excitement sped through the room, but I couldn't help but hunch down a little lower when I heard that. Next year's students getting to see my work? That would be like someone seeing inside my doodle notebook. That's practically like seeing someone in their underwear.

"Any other questions?"

Bella lifted her hand from across the room. It was easy to forget she was there, buried behind her notebook. "Do we have to?" she asked. Her voice was stronger than I thought it would be. "I mean, do we have to display them when they're done?"

Ms. Fenton puckered her mouth and tapped her lips with her finger. "Well, no. You don't *have* to. But I think it would be great for new students to see. Think of how intimidated you were when you started seventh grade!"

Bella nodded, and I shot her an appreciative glance. At least I wasn't the only chicken around here.

"I thought it might be nice if you paired up to work," Ms. Fenton continued. "Maybe with someone you've never worked with before. If not now, then when, right? Summer is almost here!" She sang happily and hopped from her desk and began spreading out the materials at the front of the room. "Before you start, make sure you pick up this list I've prepared with questions to prompt you along the way. If you're not sure where to start, this is for you." She waved a stack of pink papers in her hand. "Chop, chop, little onions!" She clapped twice and pointed to the colorful spectrum in front of her.

Chairs skidded as everyone leaped up and ran to the front. I took my time, wondering how in heck I was going to show who I was in this project. Who *was* I, anyway? Was I colored pencil? Was I a collage? Was I stinky clay? I didn't feel like much of anything without Liv here.

"Hey," a small voice interrupted my thoughts. "You want to work on our projects together?" Bella was standing by my bench with a timid smile. Normally I would have worked with Liv, but without her, I assumed I'd be on my own.

"Sure," I said, shoving over to make room for her. If the Sneerers didn't like her, she couldn't be that bad. Funny I never noticed how cute her short hair is, with tiny metal clips over her ears. She looked almost like an elf, with darting eyes that seemed to have a lot of secrets. She passed me one of the question sheets Ms. Fenton had prepared for us.

"Maybe we should brainstorm some ideas first?" She peered up at the front of the room, where everyone was clamoring for all the good paintbrushes. "We can figure out who we are." She rolled her eyes, but in the "oh boy" way, not the mean way. A smile tugged at the side of her mouth, making her even more elf-like.

"Good idea. I have no idea who I am." I giggled.

I'm not sure when I fell asleep after I got home from school—all I knew was that I woke up to the sound of Mom's vacuuming downstairs. Now that she knew Grandpa and Sugar would be around more, it was like Oprah was on her way.

For the first time in my life, I didn't even want to draw, which probably meant I was dying from some awful disease that I'd picked up from crummy math class. I always figured integers were contagious.

Things I Would Do If It Meant I Could Sleep until College

1. Play video games with Daz. Complete with all the squirming and girly screaming. And that's just Daz.
2. Juggle every one of Daz's snakes at once.
3. Take over dish duty for the rest of my life.
4. Go help my mom's friend Gail at the zoo while she helps birth reindeer babies. That means you have to stick your hand up...well, you know. Ain't pretty.
5. Never look at Zack again. Okay, this one is pushing it...

Of course, it didn't take too long for Mom to start bustling around my room, opening curtains and stuff. Why is it they always go for the curtains? It's like teenage kryptonite, all that bright light when you're tired.

"What are you doing sleeping? It's a beautiful summer day out there!" Her voice was determined. I could tell she was trying to force as much upbeat happiness into the room as possible. I mumbled a reply into my pillow, but she yanked the blanket from my shoulders.

"Not a chance," she said, ruffling my hair playfully. "If you nap now, you'll never get to sleep tonight." Darwin whistled at her, trying to charm his way into a treat. She tickled his wing through the cage bars and clapped her hands at me.

"Come on! I don't want you moping around. Why don't you come help me at the zoo if you're bored? Daz is out with Kevin, so you can help me clean the new house up before our move." Her eyes flitted to the watch on her wrist.

It's funny how parents can technically be asking a question but do it in a way where you know the answer already. And that answer is nonnegotiable.

"Okay, okay!" I huffed, yanking myself out of bed. "But I need to e-mail Liv, all right? It's important."

Important that I tell her how much she hurt me

by not showing up for our wish, just so she could hang out and go on "adventures" with some girl who has purple hair.

She gave me her best "make it quick" look and bustled back downstairs. Before starting my e-mail, I knew I needed to find the guts. To psyche myself up, like athletes do before important games. I wanted to *see* where she was.

I flipped open my laptop, hammering Liv's new address into Google Maps, like I'd done a million times since she'd left. I always hoped that I would somehow feel closer to her, being able to see the green grass near her new house.

But it never happened.

I jerked the mouse around, dragging the map back to Denver.

Liv was a whole *earth turn* away. With a girl named Leilani. I tapped the space bar angrily with my finger, gearing myself up.

I would tell her the truth.

Chewing my lip, I opened my e-mail.

Dear Liv,

I don't get it. I thought you wanted to come back home? Why didn't you just tell me you liked it there from the start?

My teeth clenched together as I typed. I sent the message and was about to close my computer when a little blip alerted me.

A new message.

My heart hammered as I saw Liv's name in my inbox. She was there!

Auto-Reply Message: Tuesday, 4:14 p.m., from Liviola

You have reached my auto-reply message. I'm out exploring our new home until Sunday, June 2, but don't worry. I will get back to you as soon as I'm back home! [end of message.]

My jaw dropped.

Auto. Reply.

She was out *exploring*?! And she didn't even think to mention that last night in her e-mail? What kind of best friend gives you the auto-reply without even warning you they'll be gone!? Auto-reply was for uncles and cousins you never hear from, not *us*.

Suddenly I was wide-awake. I shoved my computer from my lap like it was on fire. And what was this stuff about "her new home" and how she'd e-mail back once she was *home* again. New Zealand wasn't her home. Denver was! She was supposed to be finding a way back home with our stupid *wish*, not out frolicking with the hobbits. Was Leilani going with her too? Was she already part of Liv's family, like I used to be? The image of future Liv and Leilani marrying brothers unfolded in my head, jolting me with panic.

"Come on, sweetheart!" Mom's happy voice rang in my ears. "Fifteen minutes until the limo leaves!" I could hear her cackling at her own joke as she cleaned.

"Coming!" I yelled. My voice sounded hoarse. I didn't have time to think about what to do next. I didn't know if there was anything to do at all, actually. I was in a daze as I dressed for the zoo. I hoped the familiar brown uniform would help me disappear.

Mom and I drove in the back entrance and parked the car by a row of cleaning stations by the African Pavilion. I caught a whiff of the hippos instantly; they smelled like living, breathing hunks of shower mold. Something to look forward to once we moved in.

"So what do you think?" Mom asked, holding her arms open wide in front of the house as we stepped out of the car.

I shrugged. The house, which was tucked behind the lion exhibit, wasn't that bad. At least as far as fake base-camp housing went. But I wasn't about to tell her that. There was a fake thatched roof and gauzy curtains in the windows. The sign out front said "African Expedition: RESEARCH STATION." Think Africa meets IKEA.

Lions roared and grumbled beyond the open window. Mom's project was working with the large carnivores here, so I guess they figured we wouldn't mind being surrounded by fangs and angsty felines. There was already furniture, but Mom insisted that the place needed a "good inside-out cleaning." I couldn't argue, as the whole place smelled like mothballs had figured out how to reproduce and have a party.

"Can I have the room on the right?" I asked once she'd given me a quick tour. It was the second biggest one, and since I was here cleaning, I figured I should get first dibs before Daz. Mom agreed without looking up from her scrubbing.

For the next hour and a half, we cleaned and disinfected every surface of the house, including the countertops and bathtub, which I thought were beige but turned out white.

When the three main rooms were respectable according to Mom, we sat out on the front doorstep and caught our breaths. Despite my mood, it was a bright summer day, and the sound of sandals slapping against the pavement surrounded us. I'd been getting a headache from all the fumes, and my stomach was rolling with hunger, so I knew I had to make a getaway before Mom could launch into another dirt session. I told her that I needed some air and would be back in a few minutes. I wanted to be alone.

Ignoring the groups of families and tourists that had started to swarm around, I wandered down the Reptile Path. Usually, I loved watching the animals at the zoo, just living their lives. It was one place where everybody could be themselves, whether they had scales like crocs or were just big weirdos like the anteaters. It was all allowed. But today everything felt wrong. I checked my watch for the third time that day, wondering where Liv was and what she was doing. Probably hanging out with her new friends. The thought nibbled away at my mind as I walked.

Somehow, I ended up in the Crocodile Pavilion. The air was wet and dense like a rainforest, but the quiet sounds of trickling water calmed me down. I parked myself on a bench and stared at Louie, the ancient crocodile. My throat was thick, but I couldn't tell if it was from all the chemicals or plain old loneliness. I sunk my head back onto the bench and stared through the cloudy glass ceiling up into the sky at the birds. The problem with birds, I realized, is that they could fly away and I can't.

Lucky beasts.

Maybe I had more in common with Darwin and his busted wing than I realized.

I would have stayed there all day if a small movement hadn't caught the corner of my eye. I lolled my head to the side to see better.

A little girl in a very unfortunate purple dress and lime-green leggings was standing on her tiptoes, trying to hoist herself up over the top of the partition to get a better look at the exhibit. She looked about six or so, and the heel of her shoes lit up with red lights with every hop.

Where were her parents? After a few minutes of jumping and huffing, she turned to look at me expectantly. Something about wearing a uniform in a zoo made people think you wanted to help them.

"I want to see him! He's scary!" She grinned at me with no front teeth and pointed her tiny finger at Louie, who looked to be either disinterested or completely comatose.

I forced my face into a smile. "Here, hop on," I said as I walked over and lifted the little girl onto a log outside the perimeter fence, helping her get a grip on the top of the partition.

"Really, he's not so scary. He doesn't eat people, even though lots of people think he could. Mostly sausage and fish. He can't even chew his food." I shrugged.

The girl watched Louie with wide eyes, turning to face me in astonishment at the mention of Louie's food. Then a mischievous smile crept onto her face.

"Could I see it?" Her hands clapped together. I peered around. It wasn't very busy in the pavilion. I *could* show her. Plus, I had nothing else to do around here other than mope.

"Okay," I said, kneeling down to her like I was sharing a secret, "but you have to be very careful and stay right here." She nodded gravely, furrowing her brow. Kid looked like I'd asked her to guard the president.

"What's your name?" she asked while I was digging around behind some ferns for the small cooler with one of Louie's food buckets Mike keeps for educational tours every few hours.

"Ana." I hesitated. "I'm named after the biggest snake in the world." It was the first time in my life that I'd said it out loud.

The little girl's mouth gaped open. "That's so cool!" she squealed.

Hah. If only the Sneerers could share *that* sentiment. Her excitement was like a jolt of Pepsi to my tired system.

"I'm Beatrix. Mom says it's 'yoo-neek.'" Her nose scrunched up as she spoke. "But I think it's crummy." She hung her head, her small purple-rimmed glasses

81

falling to the end of her nose. "People at school say it's an old lady name."

Ouch.

"I understand." Boy, did I ever. "They're probably just jealous."

I could tell by the look on her face that she didn't buy it. I couldn't blame her—I didn't either when my mom said the same to me. A sudden outburst behind us made me jump.

"Mommy!" Beatrix jumped down from the log and raced over to a woman with wide eyes, rushing into the pavilion. She hunched over and grasped her daughter by the shoulders.

"Here you are, sweetie! Don't run off like that again! I told you to stay next to me." She turned to me and reached out, clasping my hand with a frazzled look of apology. "Thank you *so* much for watching Bea."

"Oh, no problem." I smiled and looked back at Louie. "I was about to feed him if you'd like to stay and watch."

Beatrix was already begging her mom, tugging on her arm and pleading to stay. The woman looked at her watch and gave a quick nod. By the look of her snazzy clothes, she wasn't the type to enjoy chunks of meat being fed to crocodiles. Probably more the caviar type.

"Did you know that crocodiles can't chew their food?" Beatrix chimed as I opened my bucket. I remembered to breathe through my mouth so I didn't get overcome by the stench of meat and fished out a piece.

"Now, watch." I waved the meat at Louie from behind the fence. He approached the moat with a beady look in his eyes. Or maybe it was a normal look, seeing how crocodiles tend to look beady-eyed at the best of times. I tossed the meat straight to his head. I had to admit, my aim was perfect.

Beatrix and her mother gasped as Louie lunged forward and caught the meat in his mouth. With one big, backward swing of his head, he tossed the meat to the back of his throat. Water had splashed onto us, but the mother didn't seem to notice. Beatrix was awestruck, her fingers stretched along the glass partition.

"Again!" she cried, beaming up at me with saucer eyes. She could give lessons in persuasion, seriously.

I tried to distract her with more useless knowledge. "Did you know that Louie is thirty-four years old? That's almost as old as..." I glanced at her mother, who wore a tight smile. "My mom!" I went on, "Louie will probably live to be eighty years old."

Beatrix smiled. "That's good. I like Louie."

Her mother's eyebrows raised in surprise. "You

do? Well, that's great! Maybe we can bring you back here soon to see him again." She watched as Beatrix poked at the glass wall and turned to me, whispering, "Thank you again, so much. Bea hasn't been having a great time at school this year. It's lovely to see her so happy. You're quite the natural with this." She nodded to Louie's scaly head.

I shrugged, giving a small smile. Whatever makes the kid happy. I waved to them as they left the croc pavilion. Beatrix was already yammering away about "crocodiles this" and "crocodiles that" and her mother was eagerly nodding. I was bummed to see them leave; there was something addictive and thrilling about getting to unload random facts to someone who didn't already know them. For the first time since Liv left, I had felt almost like myself. With my heart buzzing proudly, I peeked hopefully around the pavilion to see if there was anyone else there. It was then I noticed my own mother staring at me from the caiman enclosure.

She had a huge grin on her face.

"*Honeyyyy!*" She dragged out the word like a whine and rushed over to me. "That was amazing! I didn't know you liked giving presentations. You were great with that little girl!" She gawked at me.

A spasm of fear trampled down the proud feeling I had. I must have made a face because Mom started shaking her head like it was on a spring.

"Seriously, Ana—that was great. You should have seen yourself. You have a gift! You were so confident! Why don't you think about doing some educational presentations for people at the zoo—instead of all this mucking about you're doing?"

For a moment, I went insane and almost considered it. Then I realized that I *liked* the muck work. It meant I could wear a plain, brown uniform and disappear into the background. It was safe when everything else felt new and weird lately.

My throat double clutched as I imagined the possibilities. Educational staff around here not only wore nerdy, bright green uniforms, but they also had to wear name tags. Name tags! They flounce around pointing at this and that and yakking about the different animals. They were the opposite of invisible. There was no way I was going to mess with my arrangement here. Can you say, "Hello, my name is Freak Show?" Who did she think I was, Grandpa?

Of course, my mom didn't need to know how messed up her daughter was, so I brought it down a notch and said, "Um…I don't think so."

She knew better than to respond right now, but I could tell she was storing this conversation in the part of her brain where she puts things she intends on bringing up later. Possibly when the target was cornered in a car.

Can you imagine? Okay. So I didn't *hate* talking to Beatrix about crocodiles, but she's only one kid. You can't stay anonymous and stand in front of a crowd of people at the same time. That's like vanilla ice cream wanting to be mint chip. And I am *so* sticking with Team Vanilla. Between my crazy parents, my grandpa, and my reptile-crazed brother, I had to distance myself as much as possible from all that stuff. Life at school depended on it.

chapter 6

"All porcupines float in water."

—*Animal Wisdom*

How could they even find this out? Is someone out there dunking porcupines in water?

"Mooommm!" I yelled into the kitchen. "Can I use some of the charcoal pencils in your office?"

"CHARCOAL IN THE OFFICE!" Darwin echoed me. He was out of his cage, playing with some pen caps on my desk.

Bella and I hadn't gotten very far in class on our art projects. We were too busy goofing off and checking everyone else's projects, so when I got back from the zoo (and showered the smell of crocs and hippos out of my hair), I decided to bury myself with paper and charcoal.

Mom yelled back, "Yes, hun! Make sure you put them back where you found them! And no smudges or shavings everywhere! Clean up after!"

To be honest, I had no idea how to show my true self in an art project.

I pulled out the question sheet from class after getting some paper and charcoal set up on my desk.

Project Prompts: Who Do You Think You Are?

1. In order to know who you are now, it might help to remember who you've been in the past. Think about your childhood. Does any memory bubble up in your mind? Tell me about it:

I thought about that for a moment. Then, I started scribbling in tiny letters. I knew exactly which memory I'd pick:

When I was four or five, I brought Mom to school for show-and-tell in kindergarten. I'd watched other people bring in their pets or photos from exotic trips where they fed parrots or monkeys, but Mom was cooler than any of those because she was my MOM, and she got to work with cool animals all day. Her safari hat and zoo uniform looked really good on her, and she brought in an iguana so everyone could learn about him. Everybody in class loved her, and I decided then that I wanted to be like her when I grew up.

I smiled at the memory. But my stomach twisted as I kept writing. It was like I was back in that tiny classroom, smelling the plastic chairs and cubbyholes.

I was so excited when she brought out the iguana that I wanted to help her, so she let me stand up beside her and talk to our class about him.

The pen shook in my hand. I hadn't thought about that day in years.

Only I couldn't remember what I wanted to say. All the facts about iguanas that I was so proud to know got scrambled up in my head. I wanted to turn back time, so that I'd never stood up with her in the first place. So I could just sit and watch my mom like everyone else. That's when it happened. Standing there in front of all those eyes, I couldn't tell I'd had an accident until it was too late. Mom noticed right away and tried to pass it off as the iguana's fault, but I'm pretty sure everyone knew. I sure did.

I scribbled out my paragraph with one angry slash. This wasn't helping at all. All it did was remind me how disappointed and embarrassed I'd been. That was the first time I knew that what Mom did was something special. The first time I realized that no matter how hard I tried, I'd never be as brave as her. I mean, sure. Mom said that it was totally normal for little kids and that I'd probably just had a lot to drink and had been nervous, but...

Angry at the memory, I grabbed some of the charcoal. How can memories come back so vividly like no time has passed at all? Ms. Fenton always says that your art will mean most to you if you feel some emotion while you're making it. I tried to think about my favorite animals, ones that I've always loved from the zoo. Wolves for their howls, chimpanzees for their cute, pink ears, jellyfish for their long, scary tentacles. Sea horses, moose, grizzly bears, and parrots. And crocodiles. I've always loved their dark, beady eyes. Like they knew something I didn't. I drew them all with charcoal on individual sheets of paper as Darwin watched me intently.

I wasn't sure if I had a plan yet. But I knew that my seventh-grade true self was surrounded by a bunch of creatures, so I figured I'd start with that. I drew until my eyes were heavy, and drifted off to sleep with charcoal stains on my fingertips.

All math, all the time. That's what my life should be.

At least, that's what Mr. Vince said.

When I failed yet another attempt at a mock exam (I think the name "mock exam" makes sense, seeing how the only point of them is to mock how stupid you are), Mr. Vince officially assigned Kevin to tutor me after school. Until I memorized the textbook, I was on a strict diet of integers and fractions. Those were Mr. Vince's words, not mine. To put it his way, if my life were a pie chart, a huge chunk of it was spent wishing math hadn't been invented. The other little sliver was spent wanting to pelt whomever *did* invent it with cat litter. What a waste of pie.

When Kevin found me after the exam on Friday, I was beyond annoyed. Everyone else was enjoying the warm weather and the start of the weekend, and there I was doodling and waiting around my locker for a chance to look at even *more* math.

"Did you want to go to the library? Or maybe the cafeteria?" Kevin's voice interrupted my little fantasy about putting a skunk in Mr. Vince's briefcase.

"What? Oh," I said, jerking my head back to my locker search. My math binder was jammed somewhere behind my tower of emergency Handi Wipes (don't ask—I live with disgusting animals), so when I went to reach for it, a whole stack of papers and cardboard flopped to the ground.

I can't even look cool in front of the *nerdy* guy, can I?

I huffed and knelt down to snatch up my stuff, embarrassed that Kevin was doing the same. He didn't even crack a joke, and I was thankful that the

Sneerers had all gone home to their Barbie mansions. When I had finally stuffed most of the mess back into my locker, he was looking at me like he was trying to solve an equation.

"Are you okay?" He squinted at me as we plunked our books down at a library table. The place was empty, with nothing but the low hum of the air-conditioning to fill the quiet. "I know things must be crazy with your grandpa visiting…" he whispered.

Here's the thing about Kevin: he's a really nice guy. He never makes fun of me when I come to school smelling like snake after Daz hides Oscar in my bed, and even helped get rid of the crickets after that awful English lesson. He's also pretty much the smartest guy in our school. But he's so…*weird.* And okay, I will admit that he's even good-looking, with nice hair and very nice hands, which are always holding a pencil to work out some engineering/math/genius problem. But it's hard to not think of him as my brother's best friend. Especially when there are guys like Zack wandering around looking like jean models every day. Anyone who would voluntarily hang out with Daz has to be certifiably insane, right?

"Shh!" I darted a look around to make sure nobody had heard him. "I don't want anybody to know," I said. "He's staying at a hotel, so I've kept it quiet so far."

"Why don't you want anyone to know?" Kevin

asked. "I think it's cool that you're related to some-one famous." He unpacked his bag and set his text-book on the table.

I looked down at my messy notes. "Because every-one will expect *me* to be as awesome," I said. "Like he's some big celebrity, and Mom's always doing great presentations at the zoo, and it's really...hard to live up to that."

There, I said it.

Kevin just stared at me with that classic "say what?" look that guys always have.

I winced, waiting for him to tell me that, A) I was a total weirdo for not wanting people to know about Grandpa, and B) it was no secret that I wasn't brave like them so why bother trying to hide it in the first place?

But he didn't do that either.

"Everyone's good at different things," he said simply. A grin tugged at the corners of his mouth. "Daz is good at eating things, for example. I saw him eat a whole pie once, just because he was *bored*," he said, starting to laugh. "It was strawberry rhubarb, and he puked right after."

I giggled. "That is *so* my brother," I said.

"Yep," he said. "I bet you're not as bad as you think, that's all. You're probably seeing yourself from a skewed perspective."

Now it was my turn to give him a "say what?" face.

"You know, like when you're too close to something, it's hard to tell what it is. Like this." He dug around in his backpack and pulled out a book on microscopes.

"Ew," I said, leaning away. A bright green image of twisty bacteria was on the cover.

"See?" He opened the book and showed me a picture of a buggy-eyed monster with long, white fangs. "Can you tell what this is?"

I examined the picture. "Um. Something I don't want to ever see again? Whatever it is, it's terrifying."

Kevin smiled. "It's a flea," he said.

"No way!" I said, grabbing the book. "It looks like something out of a monster movie." I shuddered and handed it back.

"Exactly. Because your perspective was different. Up close, it looks really scary. But it's only a flea."

I raised my eyebrows. "And this has to do with me...how?" I crossed my fingers that this wasn't Kevin's way of telling me I was a monster up close.

"I bet your perspective on yourself is messed up," he explained. "It's hard to see the truth from a weird perspective. Maybe you just need to find a new one?"

I chewed on that while he straightened up and turned his attention back to his textbook. The quiet atmosphere of the library got louder somehow as I stared at my open notebook. I hadn't written anything yet, but I almost felt like I could actually tackle math for once. Something about being around Kevin made me feel stronger.

"So what exactly are you having a problem with in class?" He shoved his chair closer to the table and opened his notebook to a fresh page and wrote my name at the top. He used one *n*, which made a teeny blip go off in my stomach. Most people assume it has two.

I exhaled with a *whoosh*. "Pretty much everything after…" I flipped back in my textbook, stopping at the unit about decimals. "Here." I pointed to the page.

"That's the first chapter after the introduction." He stared at me, biting his thumbnail.

"Yes. Yes, it is," I said, trying to hold back a grim smile. "Didn't Mr. V tell you? I'm a lost cause. The only reason I managed to pass the rest of the tests was because Liv helped me study, and we worked together on every project. And trust me, I did not pull my weight on them either. Seriously, all this stuff"—I tapped my textbook—"is a mystery, wrapped in an enigma, covered in a riddle. My brain doesn't get it." I leaned back, crossing my arms. I knew there was no way that I could learn everything in time, even with Captain Einstein helping me. I waited for him to sigh with exasperation and tell me it wasn't worth it, that there wasn't enough time.

"Let's start at the beginning then," he said calmly. He swiped his dark hair out of his eyes and took out some practice tests from his backpack, leafing through them.

I gaped at him. "Seriously? You don't mind going through *all* this math? It's so nice outside. You could be doing anything!"

He laughed. "Hey. Remember that time I needed your help sketching all those insects for my robot-bug replicas? You didn't complain once, even though I know you missed the first showing of one of your movies with Liv, *and* your hand was cramping up." He tapped his pencil against the textbook and stared at me.

"Well, yeah. But—" I said.

"No buts! You're going to understand math if it's the last thing I do!" He raised his fist and shook it dramatically. "I mean, hopefully it's not," he added in a low voice. "But you know." He flipped open the textbook to the first chapter. "You're smart. We'll get it."

Things That Seem Really Complicated but Actually Make Sense Now Because Kevin Is a Homework God

1. Integers. Integers are just numbers, like normal,

except they can also be negative. They are the Debbie Downers of the math world. If you add up a bunch of negatives, you're going to get something even more negative. This is like starting off with getting bird poop on your shoulder, and *then* stepping in a puddle of muck while wearing your favorite shoes. You're getting worse as you go.

2. Fractions. Believe it or not, fractions are not that difficult. They're pretty much regular numbers, but they take twice the work to read. Kevin showed me this cool way to multiply them, and now every time I see them, I'm thinking of what three-fourths of a hippo looks like. Who knew?

3. Surprise fact: I love making histograms and pie charts! I don't know why Mr. Vince didn't just *tell us* they were easy from the start, but Kev says that teachers like making math seem harder than it is. He even made a pie chart for all the ways that I can scare Daz, along with their probability (yes! I even learned probability!) of freaking him out the most. (The biggest slice was hiding his videogames. The second biggest was putting Pink Swimmingo Kool-Aid in the showerhead and turning his hair hot pink. Must remember that one.)

Things Still Left Rather Complicated

1. Boys. Although he is a boy, Kevin seems to behave the exact opposite of Zack whenever something girly is mentioned. For example, when I took out my lip gloss, instead of the instant vacant expression and glazed-over eyes that Zack gets, Kevin asked to see it, in order to analyze its components. Then he suggested melting it down to see how viscous it was. I don't know what that means, but it sounds dangerous. Sometimes I really don't know what to say about my life.

I was completely mathed out by the time I got home that night. I made sure to copy Kevin's notes *twice* to convince my brain they were important. How could I remember the entire score to *Singin' in the Rain*, but not homework notes?

As I brushed my teeth and got ready for bed, something about what Kevin had said kept niggling away at me. No, not the part about integers, although that would probably be handy for the next test. The part about perspective. Could he be right? Could I be brave like Mom and Grandpa? I mean, I'd managed to talk to Beatrix without anything embarrassing happening, and it's not like I was in kindergarten anymore where people peed their pants all the time. A lot had changed since then. Geez, back then I'd slept with a stuffed unicorn named Steve. Did I need a new perspective on...myself?

I changed for bed and stared at the half-finished art project sitting on my desk, a mess of dark, angry lines. Who *was* I, anyway? I didn't want to be trapped by those lines.

"What do you think, Darwin?" I asked. Darwin tilted his head at me and didn't answer. "Do you know who *you* are?" He bobbed his head excitedly, chirping quietly. "What if you're too afraid to be who you want to be?"

"Ana banana!" he screeched.

I ignored his little dance. Bending down to pick up Ms. Fenton's question prompts from the floor, I reread the one answer I'd written. It brought me back to that day, watching Mom talk about iguanas in front of my whole class. Then I remembered the buzzing feeling of talking to Beatrix.

A flicker of hope fluttered over my heart.

Staring at the mirror again, I plastered on my widest smile. I tried to focus on how it had felt talking to Beatrix about Louie the crocodile, getting to feel that *rush* of knowing someone was learning something cool because of *me*. I stood taller and gestured broadly as I imagined that I *was* my mom, standing in front of a huge crowd. I took a deep, shaky breath.

"This is the green iguana," I whispered to my imaginary crowd. The buzz of excitement started to surge through me. Darwin watched me with interest, tilting his head. Perching my green hairbrush on my outstretched arm, I closed my eyes. Already, the facts that I knew about iguanas lined themselves up in my head, like they *wanted* to be known.

And like they wanted *me* to tell people about them.

I imagined that I was brave and proud like my mom. I tried to pretend the crowd didn't bother me, so I could enjoy that feeling of getting to teach someone something amazing. But almost instantly, the excitement morphed into fear.

That tight feeling clamped onto my chest. And *squeezed*.

My imaginary crowd sneered at me, laughing at how stupid I looked. How *weird* I was.

Thunk.

The hairbrush toppled to the floor as I flinched.

My eyes snapped open. Reflection-me was bright red, with a look of panic in her eyes.

"Ana banana," Darwin whistled. "Iguana banana!"

I shot him a look as he chattered happily. My

heart buckled with disappointment; even *imaginary* crowds turned me to mush.

"Perspective," I said to Darwin. Willing myself not to give up, I picked the hairbrush up from the floor and set it back on my desk. Darwin fluffed his feathers and glared at me. It was past his bedtime. "I need some help finding a new perspective."

Tomorrow, I thought, as I got into bed and pulled the covers up to my cheeks. *I'll get some help tomorrow.*

I knew just who to ask.

chapter 7

"Armadillos sleep for an average of eighteen and a half hours a day."

—*Animal Wisdom*

Luuuuuccckkyyyyyyy.

The manager of Grandpa's fancy hotel had a face that looked like a chipmunk and teeth to match.

"*Oui?* How may I help you today?" He sniffed and looked down at me over his runty nose as I stood there awkwardly. I hadn't realized it was a swanky hotel, or I would have worn something nicer than my old work shorts from the zoo and a sloppy T-shirt. Ladies in slick business suits bustled around me, clicking their heels on the marble floor. The smell of waffles drifted through the air, and a man in a black suit was plinking away on a piano in the corner.

"I'm looking for someone," I said, shifting my feet. "He's supposed to be on the top floor? In room 602?"

Chipmunk Face blinked a few times. "I'm afraid that floor is entirely booked by a private party. If you would give me your name, then I can leave a message." He went back to his computer, tap-tap-tapping away.

I clenched a note in my hand, scribbled with the list of questions I'd hoped to ask Grandpa about presenting and public speaking. "Please, I'm here to see Shep Foster. He wouldn't like it if you made me wait around." I tried to sound like Mom did when she didn't want to be messed with.

He laughed without looking up from his computer screen. "Oh, is that so? Well, I suggest you—"

"Ana doll!" someone shouted from the foyer. Chipmunk and I turned to find the voice.

Sugar stepped around the corner, beaming at us. Her hair was piled into a loose bun on top of her head and dangly feather earrings swayed at her chin. "What are you doing here, sweetheart? If Shep knew you were coming, he would have canceled his interviews!" She rushed over and wrapped her arms around me.

I smiled slyly at Chipmunk, who was now staring at Sugar with his jaw practically dragging on the floor. *Told you*, I fired at him telepathically.

"Sorry," I said meekly. "I figured I'd surprise him." *Mostly because I knew I'd chicken out if I thought about it too much*, I added to myself. "Mom told me where you guys were. It's not far at all."

"Well, let's go see if he can get rid of some of these vultures! Marcelle." She turned to Chipmunk. "You'll be *certain* to let Ana up anytime she needs, right then?" she cooed innocently as she dragged me toward the elevator. She hit the top floor with a long, pink fingernail.

"Your grandfather's been so busy with all the press," she said, checking her hair in the mirrored wall of the elevator. "He's been lucky to have five minutes to himself! Go on in and ignore the circus. I have to find the little girls' room!" she said when we'd finally arrived at the top.

The swarm of people inside his hotel room nearly made me dizzy. Photographers, cameras, people yelling on phones, and tables of tiny sandwiches and coffee were everywhere. I couldn't see Grandpa anywhere. I stumbled past a huge camera on wheels in the center of the room, folding and unfolding my note nervously.

"Excuse me?" I asked a man with thick earphones

around his neck. "I'm looking for my grandpa? Shep Foster?"

He didn't answer. Instead, he just pointed.

I followed his finger to the huge wall at the back of the room. A bright white sheet was hanging from the ceiling, and Grandpa was posed in the center with a copy of his book in his hands as cameras flashed around him.

"Grandpa!" I yelled, making my way over to him.

He noticed me right away, his eyes lighting up. "Ana banana!" He shouted over the noise. "Sorry, everyone! I need a minute to see my granddaughter!" He bounded over to me, nearly plowing into a guy holding a microphone, and gave me a hug.

"It's so great to see you! You should have called!" he said, ruffling my hair.

I tried to ignore the annoyed looks around us. It was clear I was intruding, but how was I supposed to know he'd be doing a photo shoot like some model? I opened the note in my hand and read my first question.

"I was wondering if I could ask you for some help," I said. I didn't want to talk to him like this, all rushed in front of people. But it was my only chance to get some advice. "Say if I wanted to be like you," I stammered. "Or like Mom. How would I be brave like that? You know, when you speak in public and do presentations? Is there something you do to make sure you don't mess up?" My hands shook as I held the note tight.

Grandpa narrowed his eyes. "Brave? You *are* brave! You're part of this family, aren't ya?" he joked, helping himself to a swig of coffee from a tiny cup.

"Hey, Shep!" a man with a phone stuck to his ear yelled from across the room. "Can we wrap this up? You've got the next interview in five!" He gave me a pointed look that made my skin crawl.

"Sorry," I muttered. "I didn't know it would be so busy. It's no big deal." I backed away toward the door, eager to get away from all the cameras. Thankfully none of them were taking pictures of *me* in my dirty shorts and T-shirt.

Grandpa gave me another hug. "It's a busy time right now, that's all," he explained. "Maybe we can chat again later? Oh! But before you go." He stepped over to a tattered duffel bag by the window. "I've been meaning to give this to you." He pulled out a tattered book and handed it to me.

"A book?" I asked. It looked ancient, with worn corners and stains all over it. I wanted to bolt from that busy room, but curiosity got the best of me as I thumbed through the pages. Little sketches of reptiles and birds peered back at me, drawn with wispy pencil lines. There were even close-up details of scales, feathers, and claws. It was *cool*.

"It's only some doodles from when I was a kid," he said. "But your mom said you like to draw too, so I thought it would be nice to pass along to you."

I paused at an ancient Polaroid photo taped inside the cover, of a young boy holding a baby crocodile with a crowd of scared kids in the background. *Grandpa* with a crocodile. A sharp pang of realization stung me like a jellyfish.

I was stupid for coming here.

Grandpa had *always* been brave.

There was no point asking him for help. He wouldn't get it. It would be like asking Sugar for help looking pretty. What's the point if it came naturally to them?

"Shep!" the man yelled again.

"Sorry, sorry!" I said, holding the book to my chest. "I'll leave. Thanks for the book, Grandpa," I said over my shoulder as I scooted to the door.

I threw my note in the garbage on my way out.

Escape. Retreat. *Flee.*

I had to get out of there.

After rushing home from that snooty hotel, I paced around my room. I'd seen some animals pace in their cages at the zoo before. Was it because they felt stuck too? Why had I even bothered trying to ask him, anyway?

Snatching the question sheet for my art project from under my bed, I stared at Bella's phone number. She'd written it in the corner, in case I ever wanted to hang out to work on our projects. Usually when I needed to escape, I went to Liv's. But that wasn't an option now.

I took a deep breath and dialed Bella's number. *Please be there.*

"Hello?" she answered on the first ring.

"Hey, Bella?" I said. "It's me. Uh, Ana. Did you want to meet up at the library and work on our art projects?" I tried to ignore how lame that sounded on a weekend afternoon.

"Sure! I'm finishing lunch right now, but I can meet in half an hour!" Her voice sounded different on the phone. Happier and bouncier. "We should work in the art section," she added. "Maybe some of the artistic genius will rub off on us."

I grinned into the phone as I swept my supplies, some poster board, and my animal drawings together, piling everything into my backpack. A wave of relief swept through me as I texted Mom to let her know where I was headed. Seriously, how did people escape their lives before libraries?

When I made it to the library, I slipped past the book stacks and found Bella at a table under a painting of a swirling blue sky over some houses. It felt *so* good to escape from the rest of the world and surround myself with quiet, safe books. Books didn't expect anything of you, and they didn't even care that you weren't super confident like the rest of your crazy family.

"Da Vinci?" I asked, pointing to the painting.

Bella shifted to look. "Van Gogh," she said. A sheepish look crossed over her face. "I only know that because I read the little plaque before you got here."

"Sorry I'm late," I said. "We have relatives visiting." I pulled out my animal drawings and spread them on the table. Bella's project was a lot of maps, with red spots dotting the landscapes. "What's with the maps?"

She beamed. "My true self right now loves maps. Something cool happened in *all* these places, and I want to visit them all." She pointed to a dot. "This is where Alexander the Great lived." Her eyes twinkled with mystery. "I think he's pretty awesome too."

"Cool." I showed her my animal drawings. "I think my true self right now is surrounded by animals." I didn't mind telling Bella the truth about that much.

"You're really good," she said, inspecting my drawings. "Why are they all in black and white?"

I shrugged, feeling the coil of sadness grow inside of me. Because I'm the only one in my entire family who isn't brave? Because my best friend would rather hang out in the Shire than with me? Because I have no idea who I am anymore?

"The charcoal seemed to fit," I said finally. "I think I'm going to make a collage." I thought about Grandpa as I laid out the pictures on a big piece of black poster board from the supply cabinet and glued them down, one by one. Moving into a zoo, going on television for his interview, everything that felt tangled around me loosened as I drew sharp lines around each picture. When I was finished, a mish-mashy kaleidoscope of animals covered the poster.

Bella looked up from her maps, which she'd cut to spell out huge letters of her name that she'd mounted on painted corkboard. I didn't know Bella that well, but it definitely reminded me of her. Quiet but somehow strong. "I like it," she said, inspecting mine. "Where are you, though?"

I grabbed a tiny piece of white chalk and drew myself in the corner, bright against the dark background. I didn't mind that I looked like a stick person—I'd tried hard on everything else. "Right here." I grinned. Quietly, I added another stick figure all the way over in the farthest corner. *And there's Liv.* I signed my name in the corner.

"Nice," she said. "So who's visiting?" She pinned the corner of her *A* down.

I stared down at my project. I *wanted* to tell Bella the truth, but I felt a twinge of guilt. Was it because I usually complained to Liv? Or because Bella had been so nice to me so far, and I wasn't being honest? I hated feeling like such a liar.

"My grandpa," I said finally. That *was* the truth. "He's kind of intense."

And comes with paparazzi.

"That's cool. I never got to meet mine. They died when I was younger."

I tried to picture what Bella's grandparents might have looked like. I bet they wore those cozy sweaters with cats on them or those reading glasses that have the strings attached. Nothing like my grandpa, who still acts like he's a teenager and likes the spotlight instead of prune juice.

"I think I'm done," Bella announced. "Ready for the world to see your true self?" she joked.

I rolled up my project, ignoring the queasy lurch in my stomach. "Yep."

I sounded more confident than I felt.

chapter 8

"A few milligrams of venom from the Belcher's sea snake can kill over one thousand people."

—*Animal Wisdom*

Note to Self: Stay out of the water. The Sneerers don't use venom, but I'm pretty sure they could infect almost as many people as that Snake.

I huffed at the mirror as I tried to fluff my hair up a little from its normal state of blandness.

How did Sugar get hers to look so bouncy? I tried twirling it with my fingers and even spritzed some of Mom's hairspray, but the whole thing made me sneeze and look like a bad before makeover photo. I gave up, shoving the mess into a ponytail.

"Ready for your last week of grade seven, sweetie?" Mom asked, sliding her sunglasses into her hair. I grunted in response. After spending the rest of the weekend hiding away like a meerkat from cameras, I didn't feel up to the onslaught of school on Monday.

"You'd better hurry up—you're late. I can drive you to school, but we're giving a couple camels a ride too. Daz went on ahead with Kevin."

I gaped outside the window at the trailer that was hooked up behind my mom's work truck. Sure enough, there were two camel butts sticking out the back.

Wonderful.

"Do you really think I want to be seen with camel butts, Mom?" I asked, sliding my backpack over my shoulder.

She rolled her eyes, holding the door open for me. "Don't worry. You get to sit up front with me. I won't make you sit in the trailer with them." She flashed her smile and hopped down to the car. "Let's get a move on!"

Music was playing loudly from iPod speakers on the grass as we pulled up to the school. Everybody seemed to be outside trying to get a tan, like lizards basking on rocks, while Principal Miller was already trying to round them up with his usual British mannerisms. This included a lot of head bobbing while yelling "hip hip." Nobody listened though, maybe because we weren't British and "hip hip" didn't sound nearly as threatening as he wanted.

I had a crick in my neck from trying to hide in the seat, squishing the cover of my sketchbook into my hair as a shield. Is there anything more mortifying than showing up in a truck with hairy camel bottoms hanging out from the back? I grabbed my art project from the backseat and tried to bolt from the truck before anyone would notice the traveling petting zoo, or worse, saw my mother. She was decked out in full safari uniform again, but this time she wore a set of aviator glasses that looked a lot like Tom Cruise's from that movie where he's a hotshot.

Jumping out, I slammed the truck door shut.

"Later, Mom," I mumbled through the open window. The sooner she got out of here, the better.

I tried to ignore the feeling that everyone was staring. *Camels and Crocs: The Silent Torture of Ana Wright*. Already my life sounded like a really bad made-for-TV movie. I was almost in the clear at the door when I noticed a huge gasp from the crowd, followed by a peal of laughter. I wheeled around, wondering if Mom had gotten out of the truck.

Oh. My. God.

A camel—a *traitorous camel*—had taken a…well, you know. It was all over the road, this huge, steaming pile of…

Principal Miller was coming up to the truck. The vein in his forehead was throbbing at first, but as soon as he saw my mom, he broke into a grin.

No…no, please.

She was getting out of the truck, patting him on the back and flashing her wide smile. She pointed up at me and waved. The crowd of students had gone silent. A few students snickered, and I hid my face. Among the faces of the growing crowd was my brother, laughing with Kevin. What? Was he missing the embarrassment gene or something? How could he find it *funny* to be part of the school's biggest weirdo family?!

I had to get out of there. *Sorry, Mom—you're on your own for this one*. Shouldering the door open, I ran into someone wearing a bright yellow polo shirt that fit in all the right places.

"Someone said there's a crazy lady with some cam—whoa there!" the voice said.

"Zack!"

My open bag dropped to the floor as he reached up to rub his forehead, which was dotted with blood. Did I smash him with the door? Mort-i-fy-ing.

"Oh! Your head!" My voice sounded like one of the lady mice from *Cinderella*.

"Hey, is that your *mom* out there?" He pointed and winced as he raised his eyebrows. She was still out there, smiling with her hands on her hips as Mr. Miller was shoveling the mess into the trailer. How did she get him to do that? Some of the students had their cell phones out and were taking pictures. Gah! One of them was Ashley. *Please* don't let this turn up on the Internet.

I tried to think of what Liv would tell me. Be flirtatious but not needy. Bat your eyelashes but not so much that you look like a crazy person. I tried, I really did, but for the record, it is impossible to be cute and flirty whenever large mammal excrement is present. When I tried to reply to Zack, two things happened. One: I said, "Unngh."

Seriously. Why couldn't I have one-*tenth* of my mother's charm?!

And two: I shook my head so hard (trying to knock out the memory of smashing him with the door no doubt) that I lost my balance and toppled back into the door.

Zack stood there, giving me the strangest look I'd ever seen.

"Do you need some help?" He scanned the floor and dropped to a knee to pick up the rest of my books.

Yes. I definitely needed help. Full psychiatric evaluation, please.

Deep breath. I had to redeem myself. "Thanks you. Er…thank you," I said finally, feeling my face flush. Were my ears red? They sure were burning.

Looking at his blue eyes, I had to remind myself that he was the crush of my sworn enemy. He *was* pretty adorable though, standing there looking all tanned with his hair messed up like that. Only Zack could look good after getting attacked by a door.

No! I reminded myself, the mental vision of Ashley's piercing glare shooting through me.

"Sure, you're welcome. So I hear your grandpa is Shep Foster." He kept looking back and forth between me and the camels past the glass door. You know things are bad when you play second fiddle to a camel derriere. He looked down at me and smirked.

"Where did you hear that?" My hands balled into fists as I thought about what I would do if Daz had told anybody.

"Oh. You haven't seen yet." He stifled a laugh, and I could feel the blood rush to my chest. Was he laughing at me?

"Okay…? Sorry about your head." I handed him a tissue from my pocket for him to dab the blood. Hopefully it was free of crickets.

"Gotta go. See you around, Annie." He nodded, handing me my books.

Annie.

Hearing him say my name (sort of) sent a chill to my toes, and I instantly forgot about his smirk.

He's so pretty.

I was about to make a clean getaway when my mother's face appeared at the door. "You forgot your keys!" she said, handing them over. Before I could cut her off, she gave me a conspiratorial smile and said *far* too loudly, "Ooh, was that Zack?!"

Might as well face it: my life was officially over.

What I Should Have Said to Zack

1. "Actually, no. That isn't my mother. My mother is a wealthy entrepreneur in Italy. She would never be caught dead in a safari hat. Say, do you like tennis?"
2. "Of course I'm not related to Shep Foster. Can't you tell by my complete inability to string together a sentence in public?"
3. Anything. Coherent.

I had assumed that the camel poop/Zack smashing would be the worst part of my day.

Sometimes I can be so stupid.

As I walked alone to my locker, the first thing I noticed was all the stares. Everybody was gawking at me. A few girls giggled and then quickly looked away as I made my way closer to them.

Please tell me that Daz didn't tell everybody. Why would he do that? Doesn't he have a soul?

"Hey, Ana—nice shorts!" a random voice boomed out, making me flinch. I jerked my head down at my shorts; there was nothing wrong with them…no random bits of animal fur or anything.

Brooke, who was somehow without her fellow Sneerers, peeked out from her locker as I walked by, with her mouth open like she wanted to say something but stopped herself. There was a distinct look of pity in her eyes.

Anger, I could take. Hostility? Sure.

But pity coming from Brooke was entirely new and it crawled over me like a scorpion. *And* it scared the you-know-what out of me. I forced one foot in front of the other, trying to ignore the dull throb in my head as I reached my bank of lockers.

A familiar tall shadow jogged up beside me in the hall. "Hey, Ana…" Kevin seemed out of breath. "I was wondering if you could help me? Um, outside.

Let's go outside. It's really nice out this morning, and we could go over some more math before class..."

I stopped, trying to shove the lump in my throat back to my stomach. People were still staring, but Kevin was blocking most of them with his sheer height in front of me. He wasn't slouching like he normally did; instead his shoulders were squared.

I gritted my teeth. "What is it, Kev? Did Daz tell everybody about Grandpa? Because he totally promised he wouldn't—he can't do this to me all the time," I sputtered. I could feel the back of my throat begin to ache.

Kevin shook his head. "No, it's not that. He didn't say anything. I promise. It's only..." He peeked behind him, and it was only then that I noticed something on the walls. A poster.

My jaw dropped as the crowd around me began to laugh. I shoved Kevin out of the way, despite his protests not to go to my locker. I didn't need to: every locker within fifty feet of mine was plastered with a photocopied poster.

Of my butt.

I gripped my backpack straps hard as I felt the tips of my fingers tingle. It wasn't just my butt. It was Sugar and I, standing at the front desk of that fancy hotel. I wouldn't stand a chance next to Sugar at the best of times, but this was so much worse. There was a huge, revolting stain on the back of my shorts. My breath squeezed out of me as I inspected the picture. Whoever had done the photocopying had the courtesy to circle my rear with a thick, black Sharpie. I knew that stain was nothing but dirt from the zoo, but in the picture it looked ridiculously terrible.

Underneath was the caption "Shep Foster's granddaughter bonds with his supermodel-actress girlfriend." Above the picture, someone had scrawled in huge block letters "LOOKS LIKE SCALES HAD AN ACCIDENT."

A weak cry escaped my throat, but I couldn't form any words.

Kevin reached over to steady me. "I was trying to get them all down before you came in. This was the last bank of lockers…" he mumbled. I noticed his back pocket was stuffed full of crumpled-up posters.

I wanted to kick every locker I could see. The edges of my vision actually began to blur red, like I was some sort of vampire on a rampage. If only I had that kind of strength, I could freak every last one of them out.

"There were *more* of them?!" I seethed.

Kevin sighed but gave a nod, pulling the stack from his back pocket. "Only a few."

I didn't even have to pretend to think about who

had done this. The Sneerers plastered my butt with its *totally understandable stain* all over school.

I shouldn't be surprised, really. But that didn't make the burning in my chest go away.

I needed Liv. She would have the perfect retaliation for them. She would smirk and wave her magic Liv wand and act like none of this mattered, and we'd laugh the whole thing off over a plate of curly fries.

But she was gone, exploring her new *home*. Grandpa had been in town for less than a week and already I was literally the poster child for being a loser. And I had no one.

Ignore them. Just *ignore* them.

I inspected myself in the spotted bathroom mirror one more time and chanted a mantra to get me through the afternoon. I couldn't miss Ms. Fenton's class. I was going to hand in my project no matter *what* was plastered all over the school.

I splashed cold water on my face one final time. My eyes looked almost back to normal, and my nose wasn't red and runny anymore. I could do this.

I stepped out of the bathroom, heading straight for my locker. The world felt different now that everyone knew I was related to Shep Foster. Like the spotlight that was normally shined on him now swung over to me, blinding me with burning light. Ms. Fenton's classroom hushed the minute I walked in. Everyone turned to stare at me, and it seemed like the air was being sucked out of the room. I kept my eyes down and beelined for my bench, where Bella was now sitting.

She gave me a small smile.

Thankfully, Ms. Fenton spoke up. "All right, my little turnips! Time to hand in your True Selves projects! I'm giving you a free period for the rest of the hour to catch up on any work you might have missed during your last week."

The class murmured with excitement.

"You're *welcome*!" Ms. Fenton said, her voice sounding like her usual happy self. I couldn't help but be jealous of her. She *never* seemed to have a bad day and didn't seem to be afraid of being at the front of the room getting attention all day.

I dropped off my project at the front, as Ms. Fenton sorted them into piles of paintings, sculptures, and mixed media pieces like Bella's. She gave me a weird look when I handed her mine, but it was probably because she'd recently seen my photocopied butt on a locker somewhere. A niggling feeling followed me back to my desk as I sat down, the dark lines of the charcoal clinging to my mind. Usually when I handed in a project for Ms. Fenton, I felt a charge of satisfaction. Like I'd done something that made even me proud. But this time? Something gross and icky was swirling inside of me.

Bella looked up at me. "Bad day, huh?"

I grimaced. "The worst."

"Is Shep Foster really your granddad?" She didn't ask in a mean, taunting way. More like she was actually interested.

No hiding it now. My mouth felt like it was filled with cotton balls. "Yeah. I have to be on TV."

Those words did *not* sound good coming out of my mouth.

Bella nodded slowly as she put together the pieces. "Ouch."

"I know, right?"

We sat there like that for the rest of the hour with our books open, pretending to do some work. But really, we just talked.

"Ana, would you mind staying a moment?" Ms. Fenton touched my elbow on the way out of art class. After such a downer day, I couldn't wait to get home and away from everyone's prying eyes.

"Hmm?" I avoided the stares of other kids as Ms.

Fenton lead me to the side of the room, but still managed to catch Bella's worried eyebrow scrunch as she left.

"I wanted to talk to you for a moment." Ms. Fenton sat cross-legged on her desk, pulling my poster board toward her. I sat beside her.

"Do you not like it?" The swirls of doubt began to mix in my stomach. I knew something felt *off* when I handed it in. But I wasn't sure why. Looking at it now, I wanted to tear it from her hands and throw it in the garbage by the door.

She shook her head. "It's not that, Ana. I just wanted to make sure you were okay with it. You see, it doesn't *feel* like it's you, you know?" She lifted the poster, outlining some of the areas with her fingers. Her eyes were narrowed. "The animals are well done, and I understand your choice to use charcoal, but…" She paused. "You seem so *colorful* in real life! I understand that animals are a huge part of your life, but the art you've made before used to be so vibrant and lively. And the way you've drawn yourself here in the corner? So tiny. You're literally barely in this collage. And who is this way over here?" She touched the second stick figure. "I know you must be feeling weird without Liv around." She lowered her voice.

There's an understatement.

"I guess I want to see that you're okay. If you're happy with this, that's fine. I just wanted to give you another chance. If you wanted it." She set the poster down again.

My lungs felt squished, like I couldn't get in a full breath. I *hated* the feeling that Ms. Fenton wasn't happy with my project. Like I was disappointing her. The more I looked at my poster, the less I liked it. Embarrassed tears pricked at my eyes.

"What do you think?" she asked, peering over at me. She was smiling, but I could see the concern in her eyes. "Is this really you right now?"

I shrugged. I wanted to tell her that my true self was a mess right now. That I wasn't brave no matter what I did, and that my stupid project didn't matter. But I knew I couldn't say that to her. She was way too nice and didn't deserve snark from me. The tiny line between her eyebrows when she glanced at me made me want to cry. All I wanted to do was stop looking at my ugly, dark project with my tiny stick person and get out of there. It wasn't me, was it? I couldn't get my mouth to work.

"Tell you what," she said when I didn't respond. "I don't have to have your grade in until next week. If you want to try again, you can get it to me by the dance on Monday. I'll be a chaperone, so you can find me there. Sound good?"

I nodded, grateful for a quick way out of this conversation. My skin felt like it might catch fire I was so ashamed. "If you do stick with this one, do I have your permission to display it with the others?"

I snatched the project from the desk. There was no way I wanted people seeing it, my true self or otherwise. "Um, no," I said. "If that's okay. I'm going to, um, keep it for now. I'll get something back to you soon." I rolled up the poster with shaky hands and stuffed it into my backpack. I'd have to think of something else. Just looking at this one made me feel sick.

She hopped off the desk and followed me out the door. "Have a good night, Ana!" She called out as I scurried down the hall.

I didn't think it was possible to feel worse than I had after my butt became front-page news. But this day was turning out to be one big low after another.

chapter 9

"A chimpanzee can recognize itself in
a mirror."

—*Animal Wisdom*

So, really what they're saying is that's one
more animal that is smarter than Daz. Because
I've seen him preening in the mirror, and boy,
it is not pretty. There's no way he's self-aware.

Tap tap tap.

The sound of fingernails on glass made me drop
my pen onto my homework and shuffle over to the
window of my new room.

Argh! "Can I help you?" I asked, squinting
against the bright sun. A group of six or seven teen-
agers were standing outside my window, obviously

thinking I was part of an exhibit. "The lion exhibit is around the other side, where the sign is!" I slammed the window shut, mumbling to myself. The smell of hay and dampness wafted in after me.

It was official: we'd been living in the zoo for one day, and I was already sick of it.

Top Three Things about Living in a Zoo That You Don't Realize until You Move In:

1. No matter how many pillows you pile over your head, you will not be able to drown out the sound of lions grumbling *all night* long like they're noisy guests on a late-night talk show that's filming in your backyard.
2. In a normal house, if you hear screeching, it means something *bad* is happening. In the zoo, if you hear screeching, it just means it's feeding time at the African Birds Pavilion. Those birds are squawkier than the Sneerers playing dodgeball.
3. Despite what I thought, the zoo is actually a great place to disappear. Who's going to look at me when they can look at zebras? Or giraffes? Or polar bears? It is an anonymite's *dream* here.

That didn't mean there weren't some things I had to get used to. So far, I'd had six random groups of zoo visitors tapping on my window, *and* the resident pelicans that have free rein of the area have decided to strut around like they own the place, attacking me with their floppy beaks whenever I leave the house. I was already regretting picking the larger room. It was also the one with the cross breeze from the hippos.

Barf.

Slogging into the kitchen for some homework fuel of milk and cookies, I nodded to Mom at the kitchen table and ignored Daz, who was running upstairs with a hedgehog in his hands. This house was much smaller than our normal one, so there were still some boxes of unpacked dishes and cutlery left on the floor. I grabbed a glass from an open box and made for the milk as Darwin chattered at me from his cage.

As soon as I sat down across from Mom and started to scarf down my Chips Ahoy! she took her opportunity to pounce.

"Have you thought any more about what we talked about?" She peered up from her papers. Funny how she said "we" talked about it when really it was all her. Did she know about my secret hairbrush iguana incident and the reason I went to see Grandpa? There was no way she was *that* sneaky.

"No, Mom. I didn't." I dunked my cookie,

swiping at a dribble of runaway milk with my sleeve. Now was not the time to look immature.

Must. Think. Assertive.

"I already told you, I don't want to do any presentations." My throat felt thick just to say it, like I was trying to swallow bitter medicine that I couldn't get down. But it was better this way. I couldn't keep pretending it was possible. I *wasn't* like Grandpa in that old picture. I let the sound of the lions carrying on outside fill the room.

"Well, I know you *said* that. But I thought that maybe you could be persuaded." She looked up at me with a sly grin.

I hiccupped, sending milk from my fingertips onto her papers. She ignored it and kept on talking.

"I've spoken with the director of education—Paul is his name—about the possibility of you leading a small presentation about some of the reptiles here. You don't have to say yes, but, hun, he seemed very interested. That sort of thing would look great on your school record, not to mention it might open up other opportunities for you here that don't involve muck work. There's even a small group coming on Sunday that would be perfect for you to start with." She put her papers down and eyed me.

I nearly gagged. "*This weekend*?! Mom, I told you, I like the muck work. It means that nobody notices

me and I can be invisible for a while. Anonymous."
As soon as the words tumbled out, I realized I should
have stayed quiet.

"Anonymous?!" she said. "Why on earth would
you want to be anonymous?" Her brow knit together
with concern. "Ana, sweetie—you have a real gift!
You are a beautiful and talented girl. You know a
lot about these animals, and it would be wonderful
for you share that with others. You also happen to
have a very unique set of skills that other kids your
age don't—that should be a good thing. You know
how to handle them, and you're so comfortable with
them, hun. I don't see why you're so worried about
standing out. If you like teaching people about animals, that's exactly what you should do!" She looked
confused, like she'd forgotten what school was like.
What *people* were like. What fear felt like. Who
cared what I *wanted* to do? What mattered was what
I *could* do.

"Mom, I told you I didn't want to!" I snapped.
"I'm not *like* you! I'm not perfect! I'm not brave!
I'm not good at *any* of the things you are! And
the last thing I want to do is prove it to the entire
world!" My eyes burned with tears as I avoided
looking at her.

She didn't respond, but the wounded look on
her face made my heart clench. I wanted to pull the

words back into my mouth. What was it about mothers that made them able to get to you? Seriously, all she had to do was look at me all concerned-like with her mom eyes and I wanted to bawl. She touched my hand.

"Sweetie, you are cut out for anything you want to do. I saw how relaxed you were with that little girl. You were confident! I think that if you gave it a try, you might find you really like it…" She spoke quietly, still holding my hand. Already the echo of my voice when I yelled at her was running through my head on repeat. I was such a jerk.

Guh.

"Fine," I mumbled.

As soon as I said it, I regretted it, and she was on me like a lion on steak, giving me a huge hug. Darwin joined in by clicking his beak happily.

"Oh, Ana! I'm so excited for you! You're going to be great. I'll help you every step of the way!" She clapped her hands together and beamed like she was watching the happy ending to a sappy movie.

What have I done?

Top Motherly Tricks: A Marvel of Science or Black Magic?

1. Mothers are capable of not only making

daughters feel guilty, but also doing so without saying a single word.

2. If your mother believes you can do something, you start to believe she may be right. Even if this goes against every single shred of evidence provided from the real world.

3. The only thing worse than suffering a mother's wrath is suffering her disappointment. In you. Sometimes I think Mom is a lot like the lions she studies. Super strong and proud, but when she's disappointed—man, that is one bitter lion of disappointment.

4. Even if you are 100 percent against an idea, your mother will somehow make it happen. What's worse is if she suspects that you're *not* 100 percent against it, because then she will *really* drag it out of you and you'll have no choice but to give in.

5. In the event above, you will not realize you have walked into a trap until it is too late.

"What's going to be great?" Daz jogged into the kitchen and opened the fridge, pulling out a carton of milk.

"Ana's decided she'll do the presentation." Mom grinned at him with enthusiasm. She turned to me abruptly. "In front of a small group, of course," she added, nodding to me and then shifting gears instantly. "*Daz*, I'm sitting right here. Would you please pretend that you don't drink out of the carton in front of me?"

He didn't respond but very dramatically leaned down to reach for a glass in a box. "Happy, Mother?" He poured a full glass and downed it in one über-gulp. "Way to go, Ana. Breakin' out of the old shell, huh?" He smirked at me.

My exhausted shoulders tensed up, realizing that he could use this against me very easily. My insides began to churn. "Don't you even think about telling anybody, okay? Promise? Especially people at school."

He winked, pouring himself another glass, but Mom shot a warning squint at him. "Daz…it is your sister's decision who she does or doesn't tell. Don't ruin it for her. We're proud of her, so let's not push her too far," she said.

"*Yes*, yes. All right. Scout's honor." He held his hand out, parting his fingers into the Vulcan salute.

I threw a paperclip at him. "That's *Star Trek*, you nimrod!"

He shrugged, digging a shiny white iPod out of his pocket and inspecting the earbuds.

"Okay, you two," Mom said, scooping up the rest of the paperclips. She disappeared off to her office, muttering about how she could have adopted. I looked around for more ammunition, but Daz had already made a pointy paper airplane from a tourist map of the zoo. It jabbed into my forehead before I could block it.

"Knock it off!" I yelled, reaching over to whack him with my notebook. He ignored me and opened the fridge again, yanking another carton to guzzle from. "I've got a lot on my mind," I said.

Already I could feel the panic start to rise again, like bubbling magma under my skin. It was bad enough that Mom had gotten me to agree to the presentation. But first, I had to make it through the week.

"Hey, loser," Daz said, craning his neck around mine to see what I was doing. "You know where we keep the corn syrup? Or red food coloring?" He poked through the boxes on the counter. "Why don't you put the nerd book away for a minute and help me out?" His smile went from sneaky to his attempt at genuine, which was the creepiest one of all, because you knew he wanted something. Milk was still dribbling down his chin.

"No thanks, loser," I retorted, closing my book before he caught a good look at my Mom-as-lion sketch. I didn't need more teasing today. "And where did you get that thing, anyway?" I pointed to the iPod in his hand. New toys for Daz always meant something suspicious was going on. "It looks brand new."

He shook his head dismissively, ignoring my question.

"Come *onnn*," he said with a drawl. "There's a group of eighth-grade girls from the school across town here, and I'm going to pretend Oscar's on the loose from his exhibit and 'save them all.'" He made bunny quotes in the air and puffed his chest out.

"Oscar doesn't have an exhibit here. He's your stupid pet," I said, rolling my eyes.

His smile widened. "Exactly!"

"You are disgusting, you know that? Nobody's going to believe that your snake has escaped from an actual cage here..." I trailed off, realizing as I said it that that was exactly what was going to happen if Daz played his cards right. And when it came to causing havoc, he usually did.

"You're seeing the genius of my plan now, I see." He crossed his arms over his chest, giving me an appraising look.

I shook my head. "Not a chance," I said simply.

He frowned. "Okay...want to help me scare some parents by the Canadian tundra exhibit?" His face lit up again as he reached around and pulled a plastic Wolfman mask from his back pocket.

I tried to do the Brooke one-eyebrow-lift move.

"Not today," I said, poking at the mask with my pencil. It was seriously terrifying, and I made a mental note not to ever fall for it if he used it against me. "Mom's going to freak if she sees you with that thing," I added.

He ignored me. "All right. I've been saving this one, but I've got this wicked recording of Mom's lions," he said, his voice dropping to a whisper. "Want to be my spy in the girls' bathroom and see how fast they tear out of there, thinking there're lions on the loose in the can?!" His eyes twinkled.

I blinked at him. "Where do you come up with this stuff?!" I exclaimed, slamming my pencil down. Go figure that I get to sit here dreading everything, while my brother, who shares 99.9 percent of his stupid DNA with me, gets to relax and goof off all day like the zoo is his personal theme park.

"Oh, my dear sister," he said, sneaking a look toward Mom's office then leaning over to open a cupboard filled with bags of crickets for his snakes. He grabbed three of them and sauntered to the front door, pulling the Wolfman mask over his head. The bloody fangs and fake fur stuck out at bizarre angles. "You'd be surprised how much space is up here in the ol' noggin," he said with a muffled voice, poking the top of the mask with his finger. "'Specially when you forget about stupid stuff like school," he said, muffled through the plastic. The toothy mask disappeared out the door, followed by the surprised chirps of crickets.

Why do I get the feeling that despite being such a dolt, my own brother has it all figured out? How can that be? I mean, he puts peanut butter on his bologna sandwiches. Surely that can't be a sign of enlightenment?

chapter 10

"In most African biomes, predators and prey must share the same watering hole."
—*Animal Wisdom*

I bet Africa feels a lot like junior high then. Only here the predators wear skirts and the prey can't move as quickly as gazelles.

Sometimes, it feels like life should stop until you feel better. You know, like when bad things happen and you have a moment of silence over the PA system at school or something. Life should do that for you when you become camel poop girl and your best friend meets a girl named Leilani and your grandpa is parading around the news like a rockstar. Life should stop when you can't figure out who you are, no matter how hard you try. Just a moment, where things don't change or don't move, out of respect.

But it doesn't.

The next day, I knew I had to have a plan. Wild animals adapt and evolve to survive their hostile environments: I had to do the same. I needed a method, a fail-proof plan to make it through the next three days of school without Liv's help. While Grandpa was in town flaunting his famousness all over the place. And my butt, apparently.

This was easier said than done.

When Liv first moved away, I sort of felt like she was still around, like a little voice on my shoulder waiting to hear about my life and help me out. But it didn't feel like that now. Now that she had Leilani and exciting adventures and all that. Now somehow the place that used to feel sort of like home to me felt dangerous and unknown. I felt alone, *really* alone, with nobody there on my shoulder.

So my plan was to disappear.

In the past two weeks, I learned quickly that if you're writing and doodling away with your nose stuck in a book, people are much more likely to ignore you. Constantly writing in a notebook is one of the best ways to avoid people. There are all sorts of crazy things going on in junior high, and the

Sneerers would find it hard to focus on little ol' me if my eyes were always down in a notebook.

Right?

Ana's Week, Constant Notes Courtesy of Crippling Fear and/or Self-Pity:

8:15: Arrive at school, narrowly miss the Sneerers on their way to the bathroom or wherever they go to apply makeup that their parents wouldn't allow them to leave the house with. (Note: The Sneerers could totally be raccoons at Halloween without much effort, given all the eyeshadow. This would totally beat their oh-so-unique cat costumes every year.)

8:30–9:20: English. Book report due on *The Hunger Games*. Really, Mrs. Roca should know better than that—we're all just going to watch the movie instead. Managed to avoid eye contact with Ashley, who sat behind me staring death rays at the back of my head. Felt slight burning sensation in my hair.

9:30–10:20: History class. Luckily I share this one with Bella, who is crazy into history and carts around ancient books and maps everywhere. Note: these books are often huge and great for hiding.

10:30–11:20: Math: reviewing session. We've already begun preparing for the final test, which apparently will be cumulative. In other words, all the stuff that I knew before for the last test but then forgot will be on it. What the crap is a rational number again? A number that makes sense? Praise the lemurs I have Kevin's awesome notes.

It wasn't until the bell after science rang when I realized I was up against what was possibly my Most Dangerous Encounter: *lunch*.

In other words, open season on losers.

For all of our junior high lives, Liv and I had shared a table at the far right of the cafeteria, against the wall. According to her, tables in the middle of the room are simply far too easy to access from any angle, making an ambush likely. The trick was to stay on the perimeter, ready for a quick escape.

I approached the cafeteria cautiously, with my eyes down. I had to consciously force my legs to stop shaking. Nothing to see here, folks. I stood in line with my tray, waiting for them to slop up a scoop of mashed potatoes on my chicken parm. Finally, I grabbed a carton of chocolate milk, paid the lady, and made my way to the table. For the first time in my life, I was disappointed that Daz and Kevin had a computer club meeting; you know things are bad when you're wishing your idiot brother was around for lunch so you could share a table.

I had just plunked myself down when I noticed Bella, sitting across the room behind a huge atlas. She was barely visible, with only the top of her head poking out. She probably had her whole meal going behind that atlas. *The girl is a master at anonymity*, I thought with admiration. Why didn't I think to ask her to sit with me? I pulled out my notebook and tried to make it look like I was absorbed in the blank page, doodling aimlessly.

"Hey, Scales. I saw your grandfather and his girl-friend at the store yesterday," Ashley's voice inter-rupted my thoughts. I twitched a little upon hearing her, and noticed Brooke and Rayna were standing beside her. They were all wearing matching skirts, which were clearly pushing the boundaries of what "three inches above the knee" meant. "Leave me alone," I muttered, trying not to make eye contact. *Just keep doodling.* Anonymous people don't talk much.

"You should have told us you were related to him. It explains *so* much." She giggled to Brooke, while Rayna watched with her usual blank look. A shot of betrayal rang through me; I didn't expect Brooke to be *nice* to me exactly, but I had thought we'd been civil to each other in class so maybe she'd go easy on me. I could use some pity right now.

"Hope you're ready for lights, camera, *action*!" She waved her fingertips as her voice trailed off dangerously in a hiss. Her eyes were cold as ice.

I shuddered at the reminder of our upcoming TV interview. "Please…" I was already annoyed at myself for sounding like such a wimp. Liv would tell me to stand up for myself. I tried to make myself feel braver. "Go away," I said, looking up at her.

"Oh, quit whining. We just wanted to get your music choices for the dance playlist," Rayna interrupted, flicking her hair and shrugging like this was the most normal thing in the world. (Are you surprised they were organizing the dance? *Really*?)

I squinted and closed my notebook. The last thing I wanted was for them to see my list of "How to Survive the Sneerpocalypse." (Step one: find invisibility cloak.)

"Yeah, okay, sure." I snorted, rolling my eyes and taking a swig of chocolate milk.

"It's true! Ashley's only messing with you. We need everyone's list by Friday," she said, smiling her widest grin as she and Ashley wandered off to a vending machine behind me, leaving Brooke standing alone, fidgeting with her nails.

Did they actually care what I wanted to hear at the dance? And how did Rayna get her teeth so white?

"Listen, Ana," Brooke said softly, "I know that

everything's sorta messed up lately, but you could go to the dance"—she paused—"plus, *everybody* is going." She gave me a knowing look and glanced over her shoulder at Zack, who was currently arm wrestling Mark, otherwise known as The Guy Who Bathed in Cologne.

I let out a tense breath.

Okay.

There was no way I wanted to go to the dance. Not only did I hate everybody, but the thought of showing up on my own in front of everybody made me want to lose my chicken parm all over Brooke's electric-blue shirt. But maybe Brooke was trying to be nice? She had been half nice to me when we made our study notes, after all. Maybe I should give her a chance, now that Liv was gone.

I should have known better.

As soon as the word *maybe* came out of my mouth, I noticed too late that Ashley had returned and had set her chocolate milk down on the table.

I should have known. *I should have known.*

It was like a scene from a movie as I watched it all happen in slow motion. From across the cafeteria, I could see someone from Ashley's table pull his arm back, then launch something. A tennis ball whizzed through the air—my own personal fuzzy green demon of social ineptitude—and smashed directly into the open carton of milk and into my chicken parm. Of course, the whole thing wouldn't be complete without chocolate milk and tomato sauce splashing all over my chest. Let me rephrase that: my *white T-shirted* chest.

I looked like a rotten tomato farm had exploded all over me. Shock was quickly replaced by bitterness; I had to hand it to whomever threw it—the guy had good aim.

Tears stung in my eyes as everyone started laughing and pointing. Rayna made a snotty click with her tongue and shrugged with a smirk, and Ashley beamed. Brooke's mouth hung open in shock; tiny droplets of parm had also spattered on her shirt but were nothing compared to the catastrophe on mine. From their table, someone was snapping pictures with a phone.

"Ana," Brooke said, her voice coming out in a cracked whisper.

"Don't," I mumbled, shoving my chair from the table.

I wouldn't give them the satisfaction of crying—*I wouldn't*. I snatched my books and dashed toward the door. I could hear the cafeteria jeering with every step I took. Somehow, Bella had made her way to the exit as well and met me at the door, wielding a handful of paper towels.

"Here," she said quietly, holding open the door first, then handing me the paper towels.

I bit my lip to keep from saying anything. I was still too emotional, and there was no way I was going to get all *Sweet Valley High* on her. Instead, we walked in silence and I fumbled with my soaked shirt.

As we made our way to the bathroom, a very British accent called out my name. Mr. Miller had caught up with me. At first, I thought he was going to tell me that everybody in the cafeteria would be punished for my little chocolate milk ambush, but his surprised expression at my shirt ruined that theory.

"Ms. Wright," he said, doing his best not to eye my top half. "I see that you are, uh, busy, but I wanted you to pass on a message to your parents, if you would." He was stroking down his tie, clearly relieved that he wasn't the one covered in embarrassment. Bella was looking at her shoes.

"My parents? Why?" I could feel the mess begin to drip down the front of my shorts as I stood there waiting for his answer.

"They've not told you?" His eyebrows lifted higher, toward his receding hairline. "Your parents are coming in for Career Day on Friday! Being scholars in their field and such prevalent figures at the zoo, we thought it would be quite fitting for them to speak to our students. I need you to tell them they're slotted in for one o'clock, right after lunch." He nodded like a proud parent.

I stepped back, steadying myself on the wall.

You have *got* to be kidding me. Why didn't they tell me?! The camel stunt and Grandpa parade weren't enough; *now* my parents had to infiltrate my school and prance around in their stupid safari uniforms talking about the mating rituals of gorillas? I must have turned green or something because Mr. Miller reached out to me, carefully avoiding the disgusting hybrid of sauce-milk on my shoulder.

"Are you quite all right, Ms. Wright? You have nothing to worry about. I'm sure they'll be smashing!" He bobbed his head up and down, and I wanted to smack the British accent right out of him.

No, no point in making things worse, I reasoned. I'll deal with this when I get home. I told him I'd pass on the message, and Bella and I hightailed it to the bathroom. She kept a spare shirt in her locker, which she let me borrow.

Genius, that Bella.

Lessons Learned from Bella—Anonymite Extraordinaire

1. Always carry a notebook and a pen. Whenever people are looking at you, whip out a new page

and start scribbling. At worst, you'll look like an eccentric writer. That means people will probably stay away from you out of sheer confusion. At best, they'll start to ignore you completely. (*She* had this figured out long before I did!)

2. Never *ever* buy food with a tomato sauce base in the school caf. It will just end badly.

3. Keep a spare shirt in your locker. In case you forget about lesson number two. Oh, and don't forget an extra set of glasses, contacts, hair ties, and sunglasses. Because you never know.

4. The library is often a sanctuary, inhabited only by other anonymites. Use it wisely and don't invite in predators.

5. Don't raise your hand in class, unless you are 110 percent sure you know the right answer. And really, this is junior high, so you probably don't. Glue that hand to your desk.

6. Most importantly, keep your eyes down. Walk behind the enemy and you will avoid spitballs, projectile food, and (most) insults directed at your clothing.

Clearly, I have so much to learn about life.

chapter 11

"Dragonflies are one of the world's fastest insects, flying at roughly fifty to sixty miles per hour."

—*Animal Wisdom*

Note to Self: Grow wings.

The last day of school was passing with a blur, and I trudged through my classes. I knew I should be happy. I'd just taken my last math test of seventh grade, and Kevin's notes had officially saved my butt. I actually think I passed! Even English went well, and Brooke sort of smiled at me when we saw that our test prep question was on our exam. But even the thrill of conquering math and the upcoming summer off couldn't save me from my parents' school visit. By one o'clock in the afternoon, my entire class was waiting for my parents to show up. Their presentation was any minute, and you could tell everyone was psyched to get a free period to avoid tests. Nobody could sit still; it was like a cloud full of mosquitoes had swarmed the room.

As the clock ticked away, I chewed my nails. I knew if Liv were here, she would tell me that I looked like a chipmunk when I bit my nails. But who could worry about that when my parents were probably pulling into the parking lot that very minute?

I honestly wasn't sure why my parents had been asked to come in at all. So far we had heard from an interior designer, a fireman (Bobby Denson's father, who was actually quite hot, no pun intended), and a journalist. Everybody seemed interesting, although the girls were definitely more into Mr. Denson. The journalist sort of reminded me of the ostriches at the zoo, all nosy and curious.

I wriggled in my seat, fidgeting with my binder. Daz was lounging in the chair beside me, describing his latest snake escape to Bella and Kevin, who had joined the class to give me some "moral support." Listening to them and the buzzing kids around me, I couldn't help the stab of jealousy in my gut. Bella liked being invisible too, but at least she was *good* at it. In fact, she was amazing. She could be a spy. She also had no famous grandfathers or nutty parents to live with. And Daz? Nothing bothered him because, well, he was Daz.

"Our next guests will be arriving shortly, I'm sure," Ms. Harris said, shushing us with her hands as she checked her watch. "I'm sure some of our students will recognize the familiar faces." She winked at me playfully. My stomach churned.

Mom and Dad were a few minutes late—maybe they wouldn't come? My palms began to sweat, leaving shiny stains on the top of my desk. Next to Daz, Kevin was designing robots. I was just letting myself zone out in his sketches, getting lulled by the random lines, when thirty seconds later, there was a loud air horn and my parents erupted into the classroom.

All eyes flew to the front of the room.

"Greetings, Homo sapiens!" my dad said, touching the tip of his safari hat like he was some sort of nerdy-cowboy–Indiana-Jones knockoff. Zack and Mike, who were sitting at the back, let out a snicker.

Oh God.

My mother joined him, opening her arms wide and letting out a gorilla hoot. I mean it—my own flesh and blood mother stood at the front of the room before my entire class and whooped and hollered like an ape. I can't make this stuff up.

My stomach retched, and I had a death grip on the sides of the desk. My feet began tapping non-stop, like they were going to make a run for it, with or without me. They had been in the room for less than a minute and already I wanted to disappear. Beside me, Daz was nodding up a storm, looking pumped.

"We are here today to talk to you about being zoologists!"

Why did they have to talk like that? They were practically *yelling*. I slide down in my chair, feeling eyes on the back of my head.

"As zoologists, we get to study animals all over the world. Some of us study what they eat or where they live. Henry and I study how animals mate," Mom explained.

A few of the boys perked up, and the girls shifted in their chairs. How could my parents talk about this stuff in my classroom? Please tell me they didn't bring video footage or this would be worse than that time in sex ed class when Mr. Grosse (yes, Mr. *Grosse*) brought in bananas.

"For many of the animals we study, one of the most important factors in mating is actually the mating displays, or rituals, that precede copulation."

Aggggh! *Are you kidding me?!*

I bit my tongue and glared at my mother, trying

to force as much terror into my eyes as I could. Maybe I could telepathically communicate with her. Mothers and daughters could do that, right? My teeth were grinding together so hard I could feel my pulse in my molars.

"And," my dad jumped in, "we've learned that some animals—like birds for example—have extremely flashy displays that precede mating."

A chair scraped on the floor. "Like what?" The question came from the back.

"Well," I could see my dad considering, "male manakins—those are birds—will do moonwalks to attract mates, like this!" He began his attempt at a moonwalk across the front of the classroom. The class burst out laughing, including Ms. Harris at the side of the room.

I bit my lip to keep from yelling at them to stop. My class was making fun of them—laughing *at* them, not with them. Why couldn't they see that? Even Daz was grinning ear to ear like a fool.

When my dad stopped moonwalking (or at least, trying to do so), my parents perched themselves on the sides of the desk at the front.

"We have lots of information for you guys, including some great audio of mating calls. But first, did any of you have any questions for us? Anybody want to get into animal-related work when they're older?" My dad beamed at the class, urging them to ask away with his open hands.

Ashley's hand shot up from the other side of the room.

Jerk. She couldn't wait to pipe in, could she?

Mom gestured to her, smiling gently. "Yes, dear?"

Ashley sat up straighter in her chair, clearly loving the feeling of being the center of attention. Before speaking, she flipped the back of her hair out. You know, in case there were any paparazzi nearby.

"Yes, Mr. and Mrs. Wright." She paused, drawing out their names to make sure everyone was listening. "I was just wondering if you could tell us about anacondas? I saw on Animal Planet that they're the biggest, *ugliest* snakes on the planet!" She looked up at my parents with raised eyebrows, like she was the reptiles' biggest fan.

I don't know if it's possible or not, but at that exact moment, my stomach began to flip itself inside out. It was also at the moment that the clock on the wall ticked to a halt.

My dad rubbed his hands together like he was about to eat a huge slice of pizza from Michaelangelo's.

"That," he said, "is a very good question!"

Ashley, no doubt figuring out that her evil plan was working, sat back with a tight smile.

My dad went on. "Anacondas *are* the biggest snakes

in the world. Not the longest, but they do have the widest girth. I don't know about the ugliest though! Their heads look a lot like *dogs*—and they can swallow nearly anything—including deer—whole!"

Ashley smirked at the word *girth*, and I began to sink farther into my chair. The rushing in my ears was getting louder, and I felt dizzy. People began to snicker around me, and I could feel the stares begin. I knew my dad didn't know what he was doing—but as far as everyone else was concerned, he might as well have just said outright that I was the biggest freak in the world. If I tried hard enough, could I disappear? Maybe I could sell my things on eBay and make enough money to move to New Zealand. Or even better, Antarctica. Penguins didn't seem so bad.

Mom cut in, "Actually, we named our daughter after an anaconda!" She seemed so proud of me, smiling at me with admiration.

That did it.

The whole class exploded with laughter. I could feel the blood begin to collect in my mouth from where I'd been gnashing on the inside of my lip. My parents, completely unaware of what the big joke was, exchanged curious looks but kept smiling.

Ashley turned to face me, tossing her hair and smirking. I glowered at her and noticed she kept eyeballing Zack behind me. I didn't have the guts to turn around to see his face.

"And what about me?" Daz called out, above the reams of laughter. "What did you name me after?" He threw his hands behind his head and leaned back in his chair.

Mom raised her eyebrows and perched her hands on her hips. "You, my son—we knew you'd be trouble from the start. So we named you after a crazy monkey!"

I pried my hands from my desk and gawked at Daz. He was sitting there happily, basking in all the loud laughter. What was *wrong* with these people?! I could barely breathe, and he was enjoying himself? Did Daz not care about our wacko family because nobody teased him? Or did nobody tease Daz because he didn't care?

The worst part was they were only getting started. Next came the game of "Guess That Mating Call" complete with audio soundtrack.

Seriously.

The class continued until my parents' time ran out, and Ms. Harris announced that our next speaker would be here in five minutes. Maybe the next career was a fisherman in Alaska and they could take me on as first mate. *Anything* to escape this madness.

As my parents packed up, I excused myself from the class. I needed a break, a drink of water, to check my locker, to restart my heart—anything— to get out of there. My parents were swarmed by some of my classmates, so they didn't even notice that I was leaving.

After a two-minute walk down the hall (long enough to get my hyperventilation under control), I returned. To my horror, Ashley, Brooke, and Rayna had surrounded my parents.

No.

The Sneerers gawked sweetly at my mom. I sucked in a breath, like I was preparing to be the one unlucky gazelle in a herd being chased by lionesses.

"Of course we'll be there to support Ana. It's *so* cool what she's doing!" Ashley gave Brooke a meaningful look.

I knew that tone.

"Totally. Maybe we can even film it and put it up online!" Ashley beamed at Rayna.

Although I'd just grabbed a drink from the fountain, hearing those words made my mouth as dry as the Sahara.

They were talking about my presentation. The *Sneerers* knew about my presentation.

I could practically hear my heart fall with a

thud onto the dirty linoleum floor. Daz, Kevin, and Bella came up beside me as I steadied myself against my desk.

"Daz? Did you…?" I was dazed. I read somewhere that in extreme pain, your body goes into shock so you don't feel anything. It's what happens when you get your leg torn off by a shark or something. That must have been what was happening to me, because I couldn't feel anything. I looked pathetically to my friends, trying to get the question out.

Bella shook her head. "No, Ana. He didn't say anything. They sort of…cornered your parents. I'm not sure how they got it out of them," she whispered. Daz nodded solemnly, giving me another Vulcan salute.

My lip quivered. Kevin reached out to guide me onto the top of the desk. "So they know," I said quietly.

Kevin nodded, giving my shoulder a squeeze. "It's okay, Ana. Seriously. So they'll show up and be their annoying selves. That doesn't have to stop you from doing a great job. They can't make you do anything embarrassing." Bella and Daz started wobbling their heads up and down in agreement.

My mother looked at me apologetically from the front of the room, while Dad looked so thrilled at Ashley's offer that his mustache was practically twitching. He swiped at his forehead with the back of his hand, sending his hat to a strange angle on his head. It occurred to me in that very moment that boys and girls live in totally different worlds. Why else would Daz not care about all our zoo stuff, while I practically have a panic attack every ten minutes when I think people will find out? I bet none of his guy friends have made fun of *him* for living in a zoo.

"That would be quite something!" He called out to me, tapping his mustache, "Ana, your friends were thinking of putting your presentation this weekend online. Isn't that nice?" He waved me up to the front of the room.

"Only if Ana is comfortable with it, of course," Mom piped up. It was nice of her to say it, but it didn't stop my blood from boiling.

I inched my way forward and looked Ashley dead in the eyes. Her fake, sugary smile nearly gave me a cavity. Betrayal, in case you were wondering, smells like dirty safari hats.

Oh yes, *Father*. Why didn't I think of that? Maybe because they've tortured me for a decade and plastered the entire school with my butt? Maybe because I'm their personal doormat and they use me for chicken parm *target practice*?! *Maybe* because I can already tell they're plotting their next move, telling absolutely everybody about *our family* and how ridiculous you look in your safari gear and how I am a part of the weird-est family in town?!

I blinked.

"Um."

What a stupid answer. I should have let them have it. But one look at Mom's empathetic face and my dad's clueless one completely clammed me up. There was no use getting into it; they just didn't understand. Already I could hear Liv's voice in my head, threatening me for being such a wimp.

"Well," he went on, "thank you very much. And don't worry. I'll arrange at the gate for some free passes for you three. If there's any trouble, tell them to call our house and we'll be right there to let you in. We're right by the lion enclosures," he explained.

I swear, I felt a part of me die inside. Ashley's sneer (masked as a smile, of course, but she wasn't fooling me) slowly shifted into a smug, tight grin. Ashley and Brooke looked at each other with raised eyebrows. Rayna—she wasn't the swiftest—was still looking at my dad with a deadpanned face. I heard a sharp intake of breathe from Bella beside me.

"You guys, like," Ashley began, "*live* in the zoo?" She lapped each word up like a cat with warm milk. I wanted to slap her. Rayna finally clued in and gasped, then smiled again when Ashley poked her in the ribs.

I felt my cheeks burning as I caught Brooke's eye. And like last time, there was the tiniest hint of pity there, in the faint knot between her eyebrows, buried under her usual mask of snobbiness that she wears with Ashley. I shot her a pleading look, but she just clamped her mouth shut and stared at the ground.

"Well, yes! I'm surprised Ana didn't tell you. We've been living there for a few days now, in one of the research houses. It's great fun—getting to hang out with the animals so much. Anyway, girls, we should get going—we've got a big television premiere tonight. Don't miss it!" He straightened out his hat.

My vision began to tunnel, and I could feel my balance waver. I tried to focus on Kev's pep talk— something to ground me. Instead, awful words like *presentation* and *Sneerers* and *television appearance* began swimming in front of me like piranhas.

Father. Shut. *Up.*

The Sneerers seemed satisfied with their ammo. Ashley had the same look Louie had when I swung raw meat in front of him. Only this time, I knew that I was the meal. They were eager, I could tell, to have their little Sneerer huddle and decide my fate. Scales and her animal-obsessed, stinky family live in a zoo. To top it off, she's giving lessons on being a loser if anybody is interested. Hat not included.

I didn't say a word to my parents before they left, and somehow navigated to my last art class of the year without crying. Ms. Fenton babbled about how she wanted us all to think about our true selves over the summer and to not forget to work in our notebooks if we were inspired. I could feel the burning get worse behind my eyes. Then, when I finally got home that afternoon, I could barely wait until I was in my room before the tears started flowing.

Compose E-mail—4:15 p.m.

AnaBanana: Liv, are you there? Where are you? I know I said I have something to tell you, but I'm too scared. And now I've gotten myself into a massive pickle and have no idea what to do. I said I would do a presentation. I don't know why. It was only going to be a few people, but then… They know. They all know. The Sneerers cornered Dad at school (don't even ASK about that) and he spilled everything. Not only are they coming to the big presentation, but they've convinced my dad that they should FILM IT AND PUT IT ON THE INTERNET. Like it's not bad enough I have to go on television with my whole family in our zoo house so my grandpa can yak about his new movie. What am I going to do?

WHERE ARE YOU? I'm freaking out. How can I get out of all this? What if I make an even bigger fool of myself on national television? HELP. I know you're probably with Leilani, but I really need you right now. Everything SUCKS.

I held my finger over the Send key for what seemed like forever, staring at my e-mail. But in the end, I couldn't do it. She was out having fun without me. She didn't want to come back. I had to do this without her too.

I clicked Discard Message and sent it to the trash. Liv wasn't there to read it, anyway.

chapter 12

"Whales and dolphins can literally fall half asleep. Their brain hemispheres alternate sleeping, so the animals can continue to surface and breathe."

—*Animal Wisdom*

I'm pretty sure I do this too, in math class. Only instead of surfacing and breathing, I nod my head to Mr. Vince's questions.

It's amazing how much can go wrong in such a short time. As if my latest ambushes and "Shep Foster buzz" at school weren't enough to give me a permanent twitch and/or the desperate need for therapy, I barely slept a wink that night. To make things worse, I couldn't figure out what to do for my true-self project. Ms. Fenton had been nice enough to give me an extension, but why was it so *hard* to figure yourself out? All I knew was that my crummy, black-and-white project was staying hidden. Just looking at it made me squirm with embarrassment. I was still awake when a loud roar of a lion snapped me out of my brainstorming.

The last day of school is always the first Safari Night of the season, and this year, I totally forgot about it. That's when visitors can camp in sleeping bags in the African exhibits with a zookeeper, and when it gets to be really late at night, they tell stories about man-eating lions and swat away mosquitoes like real safari tourists under the stars. It's a "once-in-a-lifetime experience that will live on in their hearts forever." (So says the brochure.)

It can also get pretty spooky because the nocturnal lions pace and roar a lot when it's dark. The brochure doesn't say that.

Sadly, it also doesn't mention Daz.

A few minutes after midnight, despite my droopy eyelids, I couldn't fall asleep. I was too busy scribbling in my sketchbook, fantasizing about different ways my presentation could be canceled. Random elephant stampede. Werewolf apocalypse. Jell-O tsunami.

I heard a *scritchy-scritch* noise outside my door,

and thinking it was something that had escaped from Daz's room, I peeked outside expecting the worst.

And boy, did I get it.

Daz was standing there in a leopard skin loincloth running from his left shoulder down to his knees. Mud caked his face and bare arms. His hair peeked out from underneath a dirt-crusted wig of dread-locks, tilted sideways on his head. The mangled corpse of a gummy worm missing its head dangled out of his mouth, and everything, from his dreads to his toes, was covered in a dusty white layer of baby powder.

"What the…"

"Shh!" he said, waving his hand sharply toward the end of the hall, sending small clouds of powder drifting down to the floor. His fingertips were stained red. "Come on. I need your help. You're going to miss it!"

"I'm not going anywhere! It's after midnight!" I hissed. "Mom will ground us till college! And why are you wearing a loincloth? Is that your Bob Marley wig?"

His teeth flashed in the dim light, but he didn't reply. The notion of Mom grounding us clearly made whatever he was doing that much more appealing to him.

"Here, hold this." He held out his laptop, which

had some music program loaded on pause. "Quit being such a wuss and come *on*. Did you have a bad day today or what? It'll take your mind off stuff!" he said when I gave him my best look of disapproval.

I followed him in a huff, driven more by curiosity than anything else. There was also a tiny part of me (okay, maybe a *bit* bigger than tiny) that was still ticked off at my parents for everything that had happened earlier today. Who were they to tell me to stay out of trouble, when they basically brought it to me? I gripped the laptop tighter as we crept down the dark hallway, starting to enjoy the prickly feeling of sneaking around.

We creaked open the front door and slinked out near the bushes. A crescent of sleeping bags lay a few yards away, with a large "Safari Night" banner spanning above the group of visitors below, hunched together in a circle around a small fire. Marshmallows. Little kids. Flashlights. Teddy bears. Their anxious voices echoed over the quiet path to our house.

"I heard they dug up a caveman," one kid said, clutching a stuffed elephant. Red-orange shimmers of the fire reflected in the dark off his thick glasses as he reached into a bag of chips. "Right below the extinct animals display, where the big saber-toothed tiger is! Only he wasn't *really* dead—just frozen!

Now he could be anywhere." He shivered, darting glances at his friends.

"Nuh-uh!" A little girl with a messy braid shook her head, clinging tightly to her own teddy in the crook of her elbow. "It wasn't a caveman! It was a ghost! *That's* who left behind that big pile of bones outside the lion pen! There was even *blood* on them! He could be hunting here!" Her head bobbed furiously as she stuffed a double-decker s'more into her mouth. "A caveman couldn't survive a million years frozen; that's stupid! It had to be a ghost," she said firmly, sending a spray of graham cracker crumbs into the air.

The group nodded solemnly, fidgeting and sneaking peeks at the darkness behind them.

It should have hit me earlier, but clearly my brain is leaps behind Daz's when it comes to epic prankery.

A pile of bones. The corn syrup. His stained fingers. *Baby powder.*

"Daz! *No!*" I hissed, but he shushed me again before grabbing the laptop and stuffing it in the bushes beside our house and pulling out a netted bag of white sticks.

No, *bones*. Spattered with what looked like a lovely imitation of blood.

Oh, for the love of all that is holy...

I tiptoed closer to the group, wondering if I

should warn them. They were so caught up in their theories they didn't see it coming at all.

And then, it happened all at once. Just when the lionesses let out a guttural growl, Daz unpaused his computer and I jerked my hands automatically to my ears. The deafening sounds of ghoulish wails, primitive screeches, and clattering chains erupted over the circle, and the group of kids scrambled out of their sleeping bags faster than cats from a bathtub. Screams echoed through the exhibit, and marshmallows scattered and flew in the air. Even the zookeeper looked like he might pee his pants as his flashlight dropped to the ground with a heavy thud.

But Daz wasn't done yet.

I have to admit, it was a *little* funny seeing the look on everyone's face when Daz bolted through the trees and raced away from them, his bare feet thudding hard against the ground as he flung a chaotic trail of "bloodied" bones behind him.

Okay. It was a lot funny.

"*Dead caveman ghost!*" the little girl shrieked, pointing after Daz's eerie, dusty white figure, which was already fading in the distance. I squinted to watch as he hopped the boulder past the pelican exhibit, disappearing from view. I knew he had rolled and ducked behind the vending machine, but to the wide, petrified eyes of the campers, it looked like he had just leaped from a boulder and…vanished. Even knowing there was no ghost, the whole scene gave me goose bumps.

I couldn't stop the giggle from burbling out of me as I watched them frantically searching for the caveman ghost. Then reality set in: Mom must have heard that. *Mom must have heard that.*

With one last look at the cluster of shaking kids, I snapped the laptop shut and raced back inside with my stomach in knots. Holding my breath behind my door, I waited for the inevitable thump of Dad's feet onto the hardwood. Marching out to lay down the punishments. We were so grounded.

But…nothing came.

After a few moments of tense silence, Daz crept back up the hallway. Opening my door a sliver, the grin on his face was hard to miss, even in the dark. I snorted with laughter as some of the powder from his hair drifted down to the floor. Mom would have some questions in the morning.

"Nice work, accomplice," he said, raising his hand for a high five. I tapped it lightly so the noise didn't give us away. A smear of fake blood stained my palm.

"They're going to have nightmares for life, you know," I said. It didn't stop me from smiling. I had to admit, when he wasn't focusing his prankery on *me*, Daz could be pretty funny.

"Someone's gotta teach them the ways of the world and prepare them for ghosts," he quipped. He gave me an appraising look as he grabbed his computer. "Thanks for the help."

A loud creak snapped us out of our goofy mood. Daz's eyes widened. We both froze, our feet nailed to the floor and our eyes locked on our parents' bedroom door. It didn't move.

"Think that's Mom?" I hissed.

Another creak.

"Abort mission!" Daz's voice cracked as he tried to whisper-squeal. He slipped back to his room, leaving behind powdery, white tracks on the wood floor. The muffled sound of his giggling disappeared behind his door. Diving back inside my room, I leaped onto the bed. Even though we were almost thirteen, I still felt the panic of an imaginary hand—a *ghostly* hand—reaching out to grab my leg from under my bed every time I jumped onto my bed in my dark room.

The air burned in my lungs as I waited for the telltale sound of Mom opening my door. Waiting. Breathing. Darwin stirred quietly in his cage. The house stayed quiet.

I always thought Daz had a lucky horseshoe up

his butt, and this confirmed it: Mom and Dad were still fast asleep.

Anarchy, thy name is Daz.

It was the first time in my life I had to acknowledge that Daz was right: for a moment, it had *definitely* taken my mind off everything. Maybe he was onto something?

Of course, if anyone asks where *I was* for all this, I would say I was tucked in bed sound asleep. And definitely not an accomplice to the "Ghost of Cavemen Past" that hunted on zoo grounds and terrorized children with dead animal parts.

Obviously.

chapter 13

"A large kangaroo can jump more than thirty feet with each jump."

—*Animal Wisdom*

So it would take a large kangaroo like three and a half seconds to jump out of here. I, on the other hand, have to walk like a loser human.

I used to get really nervous before getting a school picture taken. I'd take my hair out of its ponytail and try to style it in new ways, and I'd worry about what color shirt I should be wearing in order to bring the least amount of attention to any zits, blemishes, animal residue, or bad hair from my attempts at looking good. That was for one picture, that only my family would see, that would be displayed on the mantel of our fireplace for all eternity.

But this? This was so much worse.

Not only did I have to endure my grandpa's fancy-pants interview for the local news, but I was told it will be *syndicated*. Which means broadcast all over the country into the homes of thousands—no, *millions* of people dying to make fun of me.

What a perfect way to celebrate school being finished, right? Big-time wrong. What happened to the old days when Liv and I could celebrate with some girly magazines and chocolate lip gloss making sessions?

While Daz and I had taken Sugar on a tour of the lion exhibit, the whole news crew actually came into our home, which, let me tell you, was not what Mom had in mind. She ran around cleaning and dusting and wiping anything with a surface for hours before they showed up, and then when they did show up, they shoved everything we owned to the side of the living room and put our couch in the middle, along with three chairs crushed in around it. A huge spotlight beamed down on the whole scene, and someone had put a zebra print throw on the back of the couch. They wanted us to look like one big jungle-weirdo family.

"Okay, sweetie…hold still for one more second."

A makeup girl with dark eyeliner dabbed my chin with concealer for the tenth time. Apparently my zit was giving her team a run for its money. She squinted once more at me and finally nodded.

"I bet you're excited for your big debut!" She waggled her perm, and I tried to focus on not throwing up on national television. I had only gotten a glimpse of myself in the mirror before they shuttled me to the makeshift set, but what I had seen was not reassuring.

I guess they wanted to make my hair bouncier too because I had to sit inside a loud hair dryer for forty minutes with curlers and *then* they sprayed the you-know-what out of it with about ten kinds of hairspray. I should be in a musical on Broadway with this getup. For once, why couldn't I look like Sugar, with her "oops-is-my-hair-perfect?" charm?

Daz, however, had never looked more comfortable. He sprawled one arm on the back of the couch. "Hey—can I get another one of these, please?" He held up a cucumber sandwich and finger gunned a woman at a small craft services table they had set up outside our kitchen. She raised her eyebrows at him but didn't move.

I shoved him with an elbow. "Stop being such a dolt. It's a news segment. You're not Johnny Depp."

He scoffed, swiping his hair back again. "He

wishes. Hey, who's your friend?" He grinned and pointed at my concealed chin pimple.

"Shut up!" I smacked him on the back of the head.

I sat awkwardly in the chair as I tried not to touch my face or ruin my makeup. Grabbing my notebook, I flipped to the page where Sugar had given me some tips for going on television. I guess they must teach this stuff in Hollywood because she didn't seem nervous at all. With any luck, I could get through this with my dignity in one piece. Or at least, without it seriously maimed.

Sugar's Top TV Tricks to Looking Beautiful and Not At All Insane:

1. Never look the camera head-on. If you do, people could notice that your eyes are lopsided. Sugar *assured* me that everyone has lopsided eyes, and ever since she mentioned it, I can't help but stare at myself in the mirror trying to figure out which one of my eyes has decided to slip off into the no-man's-land of my face. I think it's my left one. Stupid left eye. Or maybe it's my right eye that's too high?

2. Don't fidget with your hands. You will look crazy. Sugar told me about one time when she fidgeted so much during a grape juice

commercial audition that she spilled it all over her white dress. I'm pretty sure if there was grape juice within fifty miles of me right now, I'd probably find it and spill it all over me. Because I'm lucky like that.

3. Pretend you're really, *really* interested in what your interviewer is saying. This one is super hard because sometimes interviewers are snooze-fest boring.

4. When you're not talking, make sure you keep your mouth *closed*. Sugar said that if you don't, you will look like a baked trout.

Please God, don't let me look like a baked trout.

"Okay, everybody, can we get in place please? Where did the bird go?" The producer yelled at his crew. "We need the parrot in the shot!" He waved for all of us to crowd on and around the couch. Mom, Grandpa, and Sugar had the center cushions, while Dad, Daz, and I had the chairs to the left and right. An assistant raced across the room with Darwin's cage and placed it behind the couch, so the cameras got a clear view of him. Even my parrot looked less nervous than I was to go on television. In fact, he looked downright thrilled at all the attention, clicking his beak with glee and preening under the bright lights.

My face was already beginning to sweat from the heavy spotlight on us, but it got much worse as I adjusted myself toward the camera; a huge knot was growing in my stomach. I'd take a thousand posters of my butt all over school if it meant I didn't have to do this.

Can someone's lungs spontaneously stop working? Mine felt like they had shriveled up inside my chest. I sucked in another breath; it was like breathing Jell-O through a straw.

The cameraman positioned himself behind the camera, and all of the makeup artists scattered like roaches to the outside of the room. The knot in my stomach was twisting and turning like an angry python, and the palms of my hands were sore from my nails constantly digging into them.

"Now, this is going to be great. We've already gone over questions." The producer nodded to Grandpa. "Shep, we're covering your book release, tour, your daughter, your next movie, and your grandkids—we good?" He flicked over a sheet on his clipboard and tapped it with his pen.

"We're good," Grandpa said, wrapping his arm around the back of my mom's shoulders. He looked so relaxed. In fact, everybody looked so relaxed. What was wrong with my family that national television didn't faze them? I clenched my fists harder, hoping that my face wasn't melting off under the lights and that my hair wouldn't randomly catch a spark from all the hairspray.

"And, Jane—can I call you Jane? And, Henry? We're covering some of your childhood and your own hopes for the zoo, m'kay?" More tapping on his clipboard.

Mom nodded, straightening herself out and testing out a smile for the camera. With the professional makeup job, she looked almost as pretty as Sugar (only with a lot less skin showing, obviously). Even Dad's mustache was trimmed.

"And, kids." He looked at both of us in turn. He had to check his clipboard for our names. "Daz? Ana. Just act natural. No big deal. You'll be fabulous. Smile, keep your chins up, and try not to look at the camera. Only Josie or each other, okay?"

Josie was the redhead news anchor that would be interviewing us. I'd seen her before on TV; she was always shoving her chest out like she was trying to purposely pop one of the ivory buttons on her blouse. The thing they don't tell you about these people is that "television makeup" is actually quite scary up close. The blush of her cheeks looked almost neon.

She was pulling bits of hair away from her face and fluffing it around her forehead in the mirror when she heard her name. "Ready to go?" she chirped.

The producer nodded, and she skittered over to her chair facing us. She turned to make sure that her profile was perfect for the camera and gave us all one last smile. "Here we go!" she said.

Keep it together, Ana. I swallowed down the bitter taste that was making its way to my throat and forced my face into what I hoped was a casual smile. Do casual smiles twitch? How should I hold my head? Should I stick my chin out like Josie? Or tuck it close to my chest like Sugar? The cameraman began counting, "In five, four, three." He motioned with two fingers, then one, then pointed to Josie, who jumped in right away with typical Josie flare.

"Welcome back, everyone. Today I am so, *so* excited, because I get to meet one of my all-time favorite people." She cooed at the camera, emphasizing her point with her hands. On the couch and chairs, we all sucked in a breath at the same time, like we were about to dive into the deep end of a pool all at once.

"We've got Shep Foster here," she said, fanning herself with her index cards. "As well as his beautiful family and current girlfriend."

Sugar bristled at the word *current*, but Grandpa squeezed her shoulder. I could feel Josie's eyes on me, and I was already dreading anything and everything she could ask me directly. Would I actually have to speak? What if the panic kept coming? This was going to be everywhere, and already I could feel the prickle of sweat under my armpits. I should have worn another shirt. Can the camera tell that I'm sweating so bad? Is my face shiny? Will Zack be able to tell? How can Daz be sitting there so calmly?

Shoot!

I had just looked right at the camera. Lopsided eye! Had I been doing that the whole time? Why won't my eye stop twitching? I'm going to look like an awkward serial killer sitting here twitching and sweating with a record-breaking zit.

Josie went on, "Of course, Shep needs no introduction. You've seen him everywhere—he's starred in countless documentaries, reality television shows, and most recently you've seen him on an international book tour, promoting his third book, *Wild Thing*…"

My mouth was completely parched. This was it. I was on television. Any hope I had of crawling under a rug of invisibility until I finished high school was gone faster than a bag of crickets in Daz's room.

If people could make my butt famous at school, imagine what they could do with this.

I started to count everything that I could see without turning my head. I had to focus on calm things before I had a heart attack. Things that do not throw up or accidentally swear on television or spontaneously bawl.

8: the number of sandwiches left over on the craft services table

4: microphones hanging over, around, and beside me

11: the number of times Josie has reached over to touch my grandpa's knee

11: times Sugar has crossed and recrossed her legs

3: number of spontaneous lion roars heard through the window, causing the producer to look like he was going to pee himself

0: things I've eaten in an attempt to keep my stomach empty, hopefully to delay embarrassing bathroom issues, some but not all of which include barfing

14: times Dad has touched his mustache

0: the number of times I've blinked in the last three minutes. I should probably blink now.

"That's so exciting, Shep! And how wonderful for your granddaughter to be continuing this sort of work with such passion—and at such a young age!" Josie trilled.

5: number of…Wait.

What?!

I didn't realize my mouth had been open until I snapped it shut. What did the redhead just say? I jerked my head to Daz, who was watching at me like he was expecting fireworks to shoot out of my ears. His eyes were wide and a shocked but amused grin was on his face. He let out a breath with a slow whistle and started picking at his fingernails.

Grandpa was still in the middle of talking animatedly, his eyes twinkling. "Yes, she's a wonderful presenter. I know she'll do a great job tomorrow, so you wait 'til you see her in action! She takes after my daughter, you see. Janie's always been a natural with a crowd."

I've never been hit with a ton of bricks, but when his next words stampeded out of his mouth like a rogue elephant, I knew exactly what it must feel like.

"I've already spoken to my crew, and we're filming her presentation for my movie." He looked at me admiringly.

I couldn't believe it. I'm not just saying that either. I really couldn't believe that he'd said that. I must have misheard him. Because there is no way my grandpa—no—no way my *mother* would agree to putting her terrified daughter in front of another camera for the single most petrifying event of her entire life.

Right?

Holding my breath, I slowly turned to look at her. She avoided my eyes, but I could tell the news was a surprise to her as well. She straightened herself up again and had on the poker face she wore whenever Dad disagreed with her. All business. Meanwhile, my face was growing hotter by the second.

"And what about you, Ana?" Josie tilted her head sideways at me with interest. "It must be exciting getting to follow in your grandfather's footsteps! Featured in a big movie! You must be delighted?" She held the microphone to my face.

My mind went blanker than Rayna's during an English test.

To this day, I have no idea why I said what I said. Maybe because it was the first word that popped into my head. Maybe I was so worried that my life started to flash before my eyes, and his yellow polo shirt was still stuck in my mind like some sort of fluorescent beacon of hotness. Maybe I should just be thrown in the monkey pen outside and live off bananas for the rest of my life, because when I leaned forward toward the microphone, terrified, I uttered the only thing I could.

"Zack?"

Everybody turned to look at me quizzically. Sugar cocked her head and batted her lashes, while Daz stared openmouthed, trying not to laugh. Mom's eyebrow furrowed with pity.

OH.

MY.

GOD.

The silence was so loud it hurt my ears. My eyes blurred, and the only thing I could see was Darwin the parrot bristling his feathers, bouncing eagerly in his cage beside the sofa. He *hated* a quiet room.

"*Braak! Zack! Braak! Zack!*" he squawked, his tinny voice echoing around the room.

Kill me know.

"I mean, *yeah*! Yeah. Yes. I, uh…absolutely!" I plastered a twitchy smile on my face.

I had totally meant to say *yeah*, but my brain completely spasmed. Maybe I have a tumor? An awful brain tumor hanging out in my skull taking up space in a very important part of my brain that helps me talk? And stupid Charles Darwin?! What kind of a friend was he?!

Josie leaned away from me with a hard smile and looked to the camera once again. "Well, there you have it! More after the break, where we'll discuss Shep's future plans for Hollywood. What you need to know and more, coming up next."

The Number One Rule of Going on Television Is:

1. ~~Don't look like a baked trout.~~ Do not go on television.

Five Places to Live, Now That My Fate Is Sealed

1. New Zealand. The obvious choice, but seeing how Liv is too busy with Leilani, I'd better keep looking.

2. London. I could buy myself one of those salt-and-pepper hats and go around saying "Cheerio" to everybody, like Mr. Miller. Plus, that's where Mary Poppins lives, and I could sure use a nice nanny to feed me treats and sing to me. Or one of those awesome flying umbrellas so I could travel without a hassle.

3. Oz. I mean, now that Dorothy's dealt with that awful witch, it doesn't sound like a terrible place to be. Maybe "somewhere over the rainbow" is the place for me.

4. Mexico. Not sure why this is on the list, but I do hear about an awful lot of people that go there looking for a new life.

5. The moon. Wasn't that rich guy who owns that airline trying to fly people to the moon? I wonder what I'd have to do to get on that list. Actually, maybe that guy is looking for a daughter.

chapter 14

"Dolphins, whales, elephants, and several other animal species can experience shame."
—*Animal Wisdom*

Is that Supposed to make me feel better?

I had to escape. After the interview that could only have been orchestrated by the god of the underworld, Daz and I got a ride from Mom to meet Bella and Kevin at Shaken, Not Stirred for a disaster meeting. Well, Bella and I were going to talk. I'm pretty sure Daz just heard about the possibility of ice cream.

I couldn't wait to get out of the house, away from Mom and Dad, but especially Grandpa. Mom promised me she had nothing to do with what Grandpa had said—that she was just as surprised and sorry that it had come out like that. She must have felt pretty sorry for me because she handed me a twenty from her wallet and told me to get "as much ice cream as it takes."

Nobody mentioned the word *Zack* the entire way to the mall.

Bella was waiting in a booth, looking at a menu, and the second she saw the three of us plod in, she got up from her seat.

"I'm so sorry, Ana. I just saw." She reached out to give me a quiet hug, ignoring my brother, who had already snatched the menu from her hand.

"Thanks." I slumped into the booth beside her and hung my head. I had to admit, as awful as all this was, I was grateful to have Bella around. She was like the exact opposite of Liv, totally shy and had zero advice for how to deal with Sneerers. She didn't call me a wimp once.

Kevin and Daz slid into the booth across from us. Kevin grabbed the menu from Daz, glanced at it, and dropped it on the table. He laced his fingers together. "Well. That was something," he muttered.

I scoffed. "Yeah. Sure was. Captain Charisma, right here," I huffed. I had no idea why Kevin was acting so annoyed—it wasn't like *he* had gone on television and made a huge fool of himself. He got to watch me do it from the comfort of his own living room. That wasn't in the middle of a hippo breeze either.

"I need help, guys. How can I get out of this? I will never live this down, and tomorrow it's only going to get worse." I let my head fall against the table with a thud. For some reason, my failed art project bubbled up into my mind. I still hadn't thought of something to replace the crummy one I'd given Ms. Fenton. A dark thought crept over me. Was my true self *seriously* a big loser who said stupid things on live TV? Was I doomed to feel like this forever?

Bella tapped her fingers on the table while Kevin and Daz stared at the menu. "I think I'll have a banana split," Daz said suddenly, perking up.

I glared at him.

Typical.

Kevin, who was normally really helpful, was sitting there scratching his head looking like he had something more important to be doing. When the cute waitress strolled over to take our order, he barely looked up.

"What's up with you?" I asked, poking him from across the table with a straw wrapper.

He didn't answer; instead Daz piped up. "Kev's bummed that he got the last question wrong on his social studies exam," he said, throwing him a quick look.

I gaped at him. "What? Kev, you're a genius. I doubt you got anything wrong. You never get anything wrong," I said.

He swiped some rogue hair from his dark eyes and glared at me. "Sometimes I get things very wrong, Ana."

Whoa.

Bella shifted beside me, and Daz shook his head. What was *his* problem? Did I really deserve the stink eye? I almost opened my mouth to snark at him, but Lacey had sidled up to the booth with our orders.

"Thanks, doll," Daz said, giving her his trademark skeezeball wink. Lacey ignored him and wandered back to her textbooks behind the counter.

"Let's focus on the positive," Bella said. "School is done, so you only need to face them at the presentation and at the dance on Monday night." I made a face. "If you go, that is," she added quietly, peering at Kevin. "Maybe you could pretend you're sick? Don't you guys have all sorts of jungle diseases going around the zoo?" Bella said quietly through the tension, giving Kevin a swift glance and twiddling with a piece of her short hair.

She took a drag from her Funky Monkey shake. I was really starting to like Bella, but it was weird to be drinking shakes with someone other than Liv. I might have even felt guilty if Liv wasn't off having adventures of her own without me. I wondered why we never hung out with Bella before Liv left.

"You need to pretend-catch some awful, twenty-four-hour jungle disease!" she went on.

I gave a halfhearted shrug.

"The only problem with that, Bella," Daz said, mowing into his banana split, "is that most jungle diseases are pretty serious. There's a good chance that if she could convincingly fake one, Mom would escort her directly to the hospital and into quarantine for weeks." He slurped a dribble of caramel sauce from his chin. "And let me tell you"—he waggled his spoon at her—"quarantine sucks."

"It's true. Mom would definitely know I was faking. And quarantine *does* suck," I told Bella. I poked my straw through my vanilla shake, mixing in the whipped cream. "Maybe I could 'accidentally' hit my head on something and get amnesia? Does that have to last forever?"

Bella squinted; I could tell she was searching for data in that history buff brain of hers. She tapped her mouth with her index finger. "Maybe you're approaching this the wrong way," she said. "Maybe you need to just change your strategy. That's what all the great warriors did," she said with a gleam of intrigue in her eye. Daz looked up at her and gave an approving grin.

Honestly, the only times I saw Bella get excited was when she was talking about stuff that happened over a century ago. I liked the idea of being a warrior though. I had visions of myself in leather armor with a sword.

"Go on," I said, stirring more whipped cream into my ice cream.

She sat forward and cupped her hands around her shake. Her brown eyes were bright. "Well. Take Alexander the Great. He was never defeated. Never defeated! He conquered *half* the known world in his lifetime. But here's the thing: every time he faced a battle, he didn't sit back and let his men fight. He stood out there on the front lines himself. He wasn't afraid of anything and spent his time thinking about strategy—not about fear. He didn't let fear get to him." She settled back and nodded, like she was quite happy with her point.

Daz stared at her with wide eyes, but Kevin was still grumbling to his chocolate shake.

"So…you're saying I should charge out there on a horse and hack off the heads of my enemies?" I was joking, but deep down the idea was catchy.

"No. I'm saying it was really brave of you to say you'll do this in the first place. That bravery can help you now, to figure out a strategy for *rocking* this presentation." She poked at her shake.

Brave.

The word echoed in my head as I stared at my whipped cream. When I was teaching Beatrix about crocodiles I'd had that electric feeling buzzing through me as I saw the amazed look in her eyes. I knew I wanted to teach people about cool animals, but *was* I brave? How come I never felt as brave as Mom or Grandpa? You didn't see *them* dropping their hairbrushes in fake presentations or having panic attacks in front of a camera.

And how come despite the Sneerers and Grandpa turning this into a national event, I *still* felt the bubbling excitement of getting to do it again? Was I just stupid? Or was *that* the brave part of me? I pictured a tiny seedling of bravery inside me, trying so hard to grow. Through all the fears and scaredy-cat moments I had, that teensy bit of brave still kept pushing.

Even if I was never going to be as awesome as Mom or Grandpa, I could still try. If Bella was right, then not doing the presentation would probably kill that tiny brave part completely. And I didn't want it to die.

I wanted it to grow.

"Okay," I said, letting a shudder of nerves wash over me. "You're right. I'll do it. Strategy. Yes."

She grinned and took out her history book of the

week while I dug around my backpack for my note-book. I had some planning to do.

"You'll be there tomorrow, right?" I looked to Kevin and Bella.

Bella looked at me like I had grown a third eye and twisted some of her short hair in her fingers. "Of course I'll be there."

A small rush of relief swept over me. "What about you, Kev?"

Kevin glanced up from his shake at hearing his name. "What? Oh. Yeah...I don't know if I can go. Computer at home has a virus. I told Mom I'd clean it up," he mumbled.

A dull sinking feeling took over my stomach, but I didn't let it show on my face. "Oh. Okay, no prob-lem." I swallowed a mouthful of shake bitterly. So Kevin had to fix a computer. That was understand-able, right?

Bella reached out and touched my arm. "You can do this," she affirmed, giving me a hard nod.

I had less than twenty hours left.

My strategy? I would know absolutely everything there was to know about all the reptiles in my pre-sentation. I would spout out reptilian knowledge like a fountain of amazingness and become one with my audience, just like my mom. I would ride my chariot with my head held high, using my intelligence and charisma like a blade and blast the audience with the greatest educational presentation they'd ever seen.

Yes. It would be epic.

I leaned my head back against the vinyl plastic of the booth and stared at the ceiling. An ancient spiderweb hung above me, with the teeny, dusty carcass of a fly swinging back and forth in the breeze from the vent. I couldn't help but think that, come tomorrow, that poor fly and I could have a lot in common.

Brave Ladies Who Would Most Definitely Not Be Scared of Presentations, So I Should Just Woman Up and Do It Already (commentary by Bella in italics; Daz in bold [ugh])

1. Christine, from *The Phantom of the Opera*. She's an understudy at first, but then ends up owning the whole show and sings her butt off. And the phantom completely loves her, even though he's kind of a weirdo. *I haven't seen this one yet; maybe we should watch it this weekend!* **Is this the one with the guy who wears that mask? What's with the mask? Is he like a zombie hiding his face?** No, Daz. The phantom isn't a zombie. He's misunderstood. God.

2. Kate Middleton, the Duchess of Cambridge.

She started off life as a normal person and now she's married to a prince. *Can you believe how she always looks so nice and graceful? Plus, she makes those weird fascinator hat things look classy. Nice and graceful.* **SNORE.** It's TRUE, Daz. She wouldn't be afraid of giving a presentation, so I'm keeping her on my list. **Whatever, it's your list.**

3. Katniss Everdeen. The braid. The bow. *Peeta.* Do you think Mom would let me bring a bow and arrow to my presentation? *I don't think those are allowed in zoos. Maybe we could get you a nice mockingjay pin, to boost your confidence?* **RAWR.** YES, DAZ—WE GET IT. **Oh sure, you can be all "blah blah, Peeta is sooo dreamy!" But as soon as I mention Catnip being hot you bite my head off...**

Honestly, that trip to the moon is looking better by the second.

chapter 15

"A group of crows is called a murder."
—*Animal Wisdom*

creepy. Know what a staring group of students, teachers, and parents is called? Pee-your-pants-terrifying.

Sunday morning felt like I'd somehow stepped onto an alien planet.

This time last year, Liv and I spent the whole day at the mall, eating banana splits and buying funky hair clips with our allowance. Now, I was staring at the ceiling and gearing up for what was probably the biggest day of my life. And possibly the most embarrassing.

It's crazy how stuff can change so fast.

I felt like I was suffocating when I crawled out of bed. At first, I thought it was the hippo stench of the zoo wafting through my window. But the feeling continued while I was in the shower and even when I poured my bowl of Wheaties. When I looked out the window hoping for rain, there wasn't a single cloud in the sky. It was cool-breeze–hot-sun-beautiful out.

I clicked on my computer and checked my e-mail. Nothing. I pushed the thought of Liv from my mind. She had no idea today was a big day for me; there was no reason to think she'd e-mail on her vacation. I felt a smidge stronger when I realized that Bella would be in the crowd. How funny that she'd gone from "that girl with short hair" to a real friend in such a short time.

I'd gone over my notes about a hundred times; the index cards were smudged at the edges with last night's shake and shampoo from my morning shower. I knew everything about the animals I would be talking about, including how to hold them safely and avoid any embarrassing escapes or lost digits. Mom, Dad, Bella, and even Daz had helped me run through it a bunch of times, so nothing would come as a surprise. Nothing helped the tight, twisting feeling inside me.

How to Conquer Public Speaking without Looking like a Moron

1. Stand up straight. Nobody likes a sloucher, and it's easier for your voice to carry if you're standing tall. Plus, you'll appear better looking. You may not look like a model, but you'll avoid any Quasimodo comparisons.
2. Breathe. Seriously, I know that I wasn't likely to forget this, but if I don't breathe the entire time, we're going to have bigger problems.
3. Only look above people's heads. That way they will think you are looking at them, but they won't be able to freak you out by making waggly eyebrows or stink eyes at you. Fat chance—I'm pretty sure even the top of someone's head could freak me out at this point. Especially Zack's head. Or Ashley's. Maybe I should stare at Bella the whole time? I wish Kevin was coming, then I could focus on him and not feel like a loser. Oh, and despite popular belief, *don't* picture anybody in their underwear. It will only lead to blushing and/or puking.
4. Speak clearly and slowly. If you need to slow down, count in your head.
5. Watch your hands. You don't want to get bitten by a croc, do you? The last thing you need is to lose a finger.

I checked myself out for the last time in my bedroom mirror. Bye-bye, lovely anonymous brown uniform. Hello, bright green. The shirt made me look like a limesicle, but I ignored the urge to throw it in the lion pen and adjusted my name tag.

"Questions about our wildlife? Please ask me! I'm Ana."

I held the safari hat my mom had given me in my hand. It felt like a grenade, ticking away the last seconds of my social life. I had tried it on earlier—I could *so* not rock that look.

"Hey, Ana, good luck today."

I jumped. Daz had interrupted my panicking. He was standing in my doorway with his milk snake wrapped around his neck. *He* would probably find this stuff easy, wouldn't he? I gulped down a spasm of jealousy.

"Oh, uh, thanks," I mumbled.

"I'm sure you'll kick butt today," he continued, clearing his throat.

I snorted. "Thanks, here's hoping."

"Mom wanted to know if you felt like going over it one more time. We have some time…" His snake had started to slither its way up to his ear, licking the air with its bright red tongue.

"Oh. Yeah, sure. Be right there," I said. I took another deep breath and gripped my desk chair, wondering how fast my heart could hammer before simply collapsing from cardiac arrest or something. I was about to go over my lines one more time alone when there was a faint knock at the door.

"Um, Ana?"

A dark head of hair peeked in. Kevin. He looked nervous for some reason and eyed the floor like it was made of lava. He stuffed his hands into his pockets.

"Hi, Kev," I said, trying not to chew on my lip. "What's up?" My heart made a little leap that he had even come today at all, even if he couldn't stay for the big disaster.

He took a few steps inside my room, then grinned at the fraction notes that I had taped to the wall over my desk. The ones he'd written for me, of course. I still hadn't had time to take them down.

"I wanted to wish you good luck." He ran a hand through his hair, and I noticed that he still had some equations or something written on his palm.

I shrugged, hating the buildup to this awful presentation. "Thanks," I muttered. "I really want it to be over, that's all. I hate all this." I waved my hands in front of me and picked at my limesicle shirt.

"I think you'll do great. Just ignore everybody, especially Ashley. She likes to mess with people, but if you don't let her get to you, you'll be perfect…" He trailed off. It seemed like there was more he wanted to say. I raised my eyebrows at him. Was he all right? He shook his head quickly, like he was figuring out a tough equation inside his head. Knowing Kev, he totally was.

"Ha, right. I think it would be a lot easier if I were Grandpa. Or even Daz. He's been totally chill about everything these past couple weeks," I said, rolling my eyes.

"Hey," he said. "I don't see him wearing a green shirt today. Just be yourself."

I fidgeted, smoothing down my shirt again.

"I got you something," he said quickly. "A little present. For doing this. I mean, you can have it even if you don't do the presentation. Plus, you always let me use your locker for my robot stuff, so I was thinking…well, it's something for you. I thought it might make you happy…" He looked at my shoes.

I didn't know what to say. As my brother's best friend, Kevin had been in my room a hundred times (normally tagging along with Daz while he tormented me), but the way his hair fell over his eyes made me feel awkward. Like it was weird for him to see my socks on the floor and the color of my bedspread. I tried to kick my pile of scrapped art project attempts under my desk with my shoe.

My curiosity got to me. "What is it?" I smiled and willed the unfamiliar burning in my cheeks to stop.

He jerked his eyes up to me. "Right," he said, reaching back outside the door and into the hall. He pulled back a small paper bag and half handed, half thrust it into my hands. It was light and flat, with the brown paper crumpled at the top like it had been opened and closed over and over again.

A grin took over my face as I unrolled the top. Something flat was inside. I couldn't hide my delight as I pulled it out: a leather journal, beautiful and brown, was embossed with my name. It looked a lot like Grandpa's old sketchbook, except with no stains or tattered corners.

He spoke before I could. "I see you writing and sketching a lot at school. In that crummy notebook." He pointed at my desk, where a stack of my books had toppled onto my exam notes. Sure enough, my notebook was on top, sitting next to Grandpa's; I couldn't imagine getting through the past couple weeks without it to help me hide from the Sneerers. I was sort of floored that Kevin even noticed.

"Kev—that's so nice." I put the bag down and ran my hand across the surface of the book. "Ana" was embossed in gold, written in an old style of calligraphy. The pages were a light butter yellow. It looked like the kind of book that anything would look epic in. Already I was thinking about what to write on the first page.

He grinned. "No lines either." He grabbed the top of the journal and opened to a page. "I noticed you don't use them too much when we were making math notes." He smiled gently.

"Hah! Excellent." I bit my lip, embarrassed. "This is really great…" I tried to think of a way to thank him, but my words seemed garbled in my mouth. "Thanks so much," was all that came out.

He seemed happy with this and rolled back on his heels. I looked down at the journal again, but it was only because I was too uneasy to look him in the eyes.

"So you have to go fix your mom's computer now?" I asked. My fingers traced the cover of the journal. I didn't want him to leave but knew that saying it would probably put him on the spot. Since when were there specks of yellow in his eyes?

He furrowed his brow and peered down at me. "Nah," he said, giving me a small smile. "It can wait. I don't want to have to wait for the movie to come out to see how you did."

I laughed, but the flutter in my stomach was going full tilt. The thought of him in the audience somehow made me feel safer. He waved a quick good-bye and headed back to Daz's room, where I could only assume the two of them were going to enjoy their future lack of movie appearances in leisurely joy.

I will never understand boys.

As I trudged down the stairs to the kitchen and my waiting parents, my face began to tingle, this time out of fear. I wanted nothing more than to escape into my room for the rest of the day to sketch in my new journal, but I wasn't that lucky.

In the kitchen, my parents looked so relaxed. Mom handed me a glass of water. Grandpa was already outside "working the crowd" (his words, not mine), so Sugar was here for moral support and sitting with my parents, filing her nails.

"Okay, so," I announced, "you guys mind if I do the introduction once more? To make sure I've got it?" I took a deep breath. Already I could feel a loud rushing in my ears, like there was a whole ocean inside my head trying to crash out.

My mom smiled. "Of course, honey. We're all ears." She clasped her hands together and set them in her lap. Dad looked up from his coffee.

"All ears!" Darwin cackled in his cage.

I tried to remember what the index cards said— stand up straight. Breathe. Something about reptiles. Then, as quickly as I could envision the cards in front of me, they disappeared. There were too many eyes on me. All the stupid rules about where to look and how to talk were gone. I couldn't even picture the animals I'd be working with. Monkeys? Koalas?

I lurched forward, leaning on the counter. I could feel it happening already.

The tiny seedling of bravery felt like it was withering away inside of me.

I was completely blank.

My parents and Sugar stared at me, probably wondering why my mouth was open and nothing was coming out of it. The room spun as Ashley's sneer and Zack's smirk popped into my head, tangled up with memories of that horrible day in kindergarten when I'd embarrassed myself so much it *hurt*. Suddenly I felt like crying. My hands, which were so still a moment earlier, began to tremble.

Then the weight from the past two weeks came crashing over me, nearly making my knees buckle. Liv not wanting to come home. Ashley. *Zack*. The poster of my butt. The look on Kevin's face after my television mishap. So many reasons to run and hide.

And now I was putting myself out there *again*. I must be seriously messed up. Psych ward, puffy walls, straitjacket messed up, like I see in the movies.

"I can't do this, you guys," I broke down, stammering. "I—I completely forget everything." Tears stung at the back of my eyes, but I refused to let them out. The room was swimming in front of me as I grappled to stay vertical.

Mom leaped up from the table, giving Dad the eye to come and join her. They both wrapped their arms around me. Sugar frowned empathetically and touched her hand to her chest.

"Oh, darlin'…" she whispered.

I wanted to disappear I felt so stupid. Why couldn't I just be a regular kid, looking forward to summer with my best friend and stupid movies and a *non-zoo house* with non-famous relatives without this stupid lime-green shirt on? It felt like someone was crushing my heart with their fist.

"Honey. Of *course* you can do this! You're getting cold feet! It's natural. Normal." Mom stroked my hair. It made me feel about three years old, but I was too strung out to pull away.

"Normal!" I shrieked. "Mom, I'm *anything* but normal!"

My dad piped in, looking hurt. "Hey, what's that supposed to mean?" he said, backing away to let my mom handle the hugging portion of the intervention.

I glared at them. I didn't want to make things worse, but I couldn't help it. I wanted to lash out.

"Why did you have to name me after a snake?" The question sprang from my mouth. I knew I sounded whiny, but I really didn't understand. My name felt like an inescapable reminder of how bizarre this family is. Like a bold stamp on my face that labeled me, that I'd never be able to rub off. They were twelve once; how could they *not* know that some stinking reptile wasn't exactly a great inspiration for a baby name.

I didn't even bother to let them answer; the flood of tears had started. "Practically my whole class will be there, waiting for me to mess up, not to mention Grandpa's stupid *movie crew* will have their cameras up my nose, and absolutely *nobody* cares about how any of this makes me feel, and no matter what I do I *never* feel brave for real!" I stormed around the kitchen, avoiding eye contact while tears fell onto my lime-green shirt. Darwin ruffled his feathers and clawed at his cage door, sensing that I was upset.

Mom was silent but gave me a small nod of understanding. Dad was running his hands through his hair, clearly thrown off by my crying. Sugar looked like she wanted to jump up from her chair and wrap me in a hug.

"Honey. You want to know why we named you after that snake?" she asked quietly, folding her hands on her lap.

I stared at her, squinting through the blur of tears.

"Your father and I were working together, in

South America. This was long before you were born. Actually, it was before we even got together. We were on a team together looking for anacondas, and…well, I was pretty new at the whole field research thing."

I nodded with a jerk of my head, partially distracted by the image of my mom being not capable of something. Dad's lips began to curl up in a small smile under his mustache.

"We found the snake we were looking for, but when we managed to wrangle it and tag him," she paused, embarrassment in her eyes. "Well, I couldn't hold on, and I fell right off the boat into the water. Your father, he didn't even hesitate." She grinned. "He jumped right in the water after me, got me away from the snake, and hauled me out." I could tell she was amused at the memory because her eyes crinkled a little. Sugar made a teeny cooing noise.

"That was how we fell in love, Ana. If it wasn't for that snake—and, yes, he was a big and ugly snake—we probably wouldn't have gotten together. And *you* probably wouldn't be here. We wanted to name our daughter after what started it all."

I looked at my dad, who was nodding, a goofball look on his face.

Huh.

A sigh whooshed out of my mouth, like the rush

of air from a deflated tire. I admit, I was sort of wishing that my parents had fallen in love over some beautiful, exotic bird instead of the snake, but really, that was kind of…*sweet*.

I dried my eyes, not knowing what to say.

My dad spoke. "Even if you don't like your name, one day you'll see that you can't let other people make you feel bad. There's a saying"—he cleared his throat and put his hand in the air—"if you stand tall, you'll be shot at. If you stoop down, you'll get stepped on. Everybody faces this, Ana. It's up to you to decide what you want and who you are. One day, honey, you'll learn that what other people think doesn't matter. What makes you happy, that's what's important."

Mom reached an arm around the back of his shoulder. I knew they weren't trying to get all PSA on me, but I couldn't help but stifle a small grin.

"Now," Mom said, putting her arm around my shoulder. "Do you still want to do this, Ana? Say the word and I'll get you out." She turned to stare at me head on.

I swallowed hard and started to shake my head. I felt numb inside, like my body had felt too many emotions in the past month and had put up a "Come Back Later" sign. I didn't know what to think or what to feel; I was just totally empty. Mom squeezed my shoulders and gave Dad a quick look. I knew she was trying not to look disappointed in me. And maybe she wasn't.

Maybe it wasn't *her* disappointment I was feeling at all.

"I don't know," I mumbled.

That's when the phone rang.

Mom's eyes softened as she looked at the caller ID. Her voice was sympathetic. "It's Liv, dear. Should I say you're busy?"

chapter 16

"If you keep a goldfish in a dark room, it
will become pale."

—*Animal Wisdom*

I jumped in surprise.

Riiiinnng…

"Liv?" My hands started to shake. "She's away
touring right now, why would she call?" The ring-
ing continued as Dad looked confused.

"Is someone going to pick that up?" he asked.

I nodded. "I got it," I said, reaching for the phone.
Taking a deep breath, I clicked it on.

Liv was on the other end. "Hello? Ana? It's me.
What the heck is all this I'm reading about you
giving a presentation?" Her words came out in one
long sentence. I could hear the grin in her voice.

I gasped. "What? Hi! Where? Did the Sneerers
blog about it or something?"

Liv giggled. "No, monkey butt! It's in the zoo newsletter. I signed up years ago, 'member? It says, 'Ana Wright, granddaughter of Shep Foster, will be hosting a presentation with a select group of reptiles, on Sunday, June 7,'" she recited. "That's *you*, last time I checked!"

I exhaled. "Oh. Well, yeah," I said. "I mean. It's true. Or it was. I'm not so sure anymore," I admitted.

She shrieked. "How could you not tell me, Ana?! Have you been taken over by a martian?! I want to *see* it! Can you get someone to film it, maybe?" she asked. Frustration stabbed at me. How could she act so normal when she'd basically chosen New Zealand over me?

I grimaced. "Well, I'm pretty sure Ashley will have it up on the Internet if she has her way," I groaned. I gripped my hands into fists.

"Hah, of course she will," Liv said flippantly. The tinny phone line crackled in my ear.

"So," I said, filling the long pause between us. "I hear you're liking it there."

Liv sighed. "I know you're mad at me about the cupcake wish," she said. "You know I don't want to make you upset, I just…I like it here, you know? It's like being on an adventure."

I nodded silently.

"And we are still best friends," she said. She began

to giggle. "It seems like you're having a perfectly fine time without me, Miss Fancy Presentations!"

I frowned. "It hasn't exactly been easy here lately. Sometimes it feels like I have no idea who I am without you," I said. I looked down at my bright green shirt. "A lot has changed."

"I know," she said quietly. "I feel the same way. But I don't want you to hate me for wanting to stay here."

Shaking my head, I knew the answer to that. No matter how much I wanted Liv back, I didn't want her to be sad where she was. "No, I don't. I'm really glad you're happy there."

And I was. This whole best friend living far away thing was going to take a little more getting used to.

"So, you'd better go get ready, huh?" she said suddenly. "For your presentation."

I shook my head. "Actually, I'm not too sure if I'm going to do it. There's a lot of people out there, and, well, I don't think I'm ready," I said.

She was silent for a minute. "That's okay. There's always another crocodile, right?"

"Thanks, Liv. I'll talk to you once you're back from your tour," I said. I felt like giving her a hug, but the best we had was the phone. "Thanks for calling. I'm sorry for being weird about you wanting to stay."

"Me too, for messing us up," she said. "I'll send

you a postcard from Lake Taupo! That's our next stop," she said happily. "My dad is going skydiving!"

I tried to picture quiet Mr. Reed doing something as crazy as skydiving. I guess everybody was changing, even the grown-ups.

When we hung up, I wandered back into the kitchen.

"How was she? Loving her new home, I bet?" Mom smiled. I knew she was avoiding mentioning my presentation.

I nodded. "Yeah," I said. "She loves it there."

A sharp knock on the door alerted us all, and Grandpa strode in with a grin, wearing one of his brightest Hawaiian shirts yet. "Crowd's ready, Janie—hey, what's wrong, Banana?" he said. His eyebrows knit together as he took in my face; I'm sure I looked like a splotchy mess. It had been quite the morning of bawling and confessing. I was ready for a nap already.

"Ana doesn't feel up to the presentation, Dad," Mom said gently.

He looked at me for a beat, then gave a soft smile. "Oh! Well…that's…I understand. Mind if I talk to her for a second then?" He held out his hand to me, ignoring Mom's questioning look.

"It's okay, Mom," I said, reluctantly grabbing his hand and following him away from everybody's stares.

He put his arm around my shoulders as he walked

down the hall. "Tough day, huh?" he said, peeking into my room, seemingly looking for something. His eyes lit up when he saw my desk.

"I just don't think I have it in me, Grandpa. I'm really sorry," I said. The words felt so heavy coming out of my mouth. I wished I could drag them back in. I didn't want to disappoint him either.

"Hey, that's no problem," he said. "Say, did you ever get to take a look at this?" He walked over and picked up his old sketchbook, sitting next to mine on my desk. He flipped through the pages wistfully as I nodded slowly.

"Um, yeah. I did. You were good," I mumbled. Guilt flushed over me; I didn't want to tell him that I had a hard time looking at his sketchbook. That little boy holding the crocodile in the picture seemed to have everything I didn't.

Talent. Guts. *Especially* guts. I didn't need another reminder.

A laugh escaped his mouth as he tilted his head to examine the inside of the front cover. "I'd forgotten about this picture!" he said, pulling me over to see it.

"How old were you there?" I asked absently. I wanted something—anything—to distract me from the waterworks that were threatening to show up again.

He brought the picture closer to his face

and squinted. "Oh, I'd guess maybe seven or eight. Look how terrified I am at that croc!" He chuckled.

I narrowed my eyes and looked at the picture again, examining the messy blond boy holding a young crocodile, with a crowd of kids looking on in awe. "You don't look scared to me," I said. Maybe that's why it was so hard to live up to this family. The bar was so high. Shame crept over me again as I thought of my parents, who were probably trying to scramble to fill my presentation.

"Ana." He paused, looking down at me. "What exactly do you see in this picture?" His blue eyes were full of questions.

I shrugged. "I see you as a little kid, holding a croc." Why was he trying to rub it in?

The corner of his lips turned upward, and for the first time, I saw where my mom had gotten her mischievous twinkling eyes.

"Ana," he said, pointing to the young blond boy. "That's not me."

I stiffened. "What?"

I watched as his finger moved on the picture, not to point at the small blond boy with the croc, but to one of the onlookers in the crowd around him. A chubby boy with a buzz cut looked back at me, nearly invisible in the group. It was clear he was enamored with the crocodile, but you could see a distinct fear in his wide eyes. *Familiar eyes.*

My grandpa.

Part of the crowd. In the background.

Scared.

"No!" I said, looking up at him with surprise. "You were scared!" *And chubby!* I wanted to add.

He laughed. "This was my first visit to a zoo. This kid"—he tapped the blond boy again—"was the zookeeper's son. It took me another two years to even get the guts to pick up a croc of my own!" The corners of his eyes crinkled.

Wow.

I didn't even know what to say.

"Everybody gets scared, Banana," he said softly.

I nodded, still trying to wrap my brain around the idea of Grandpa being a wallflower. Well, a zooflower.

"I pretty much feel scared all the time," I muttered. "I'm not brave like you and Mom."

He nodded. "I know what you mean. But you know what I've learned about bravery? It's not something you just *have*. It's something you choose. And the more you choose it, the more it grows. That's what I try to remember when I get scared."

I thought about the little seedling of bravery that

felt crippled and small in my chest. Bending and breaking to the panic I felt.

"All you have to do is live for you," he said simply. "If you want something, and it scares you…well, you're the one who gets to choose whether that stops you. Nobody else. And sometimes, the stuff that scares us is the stuff that means the most to us."

I gulped. A buzzing feeling was beginning to spread over my chest and throat. Somewhere, deep underneath the limesicle coating of bitterness and fear, his words really hit me. The brave part of me was shuddering and forcing its way through. *It* knew what I wanted to do. Even if the rest of me hadn't caught up yet.

"Grandpa," I said quietly, as he closed the book and set it back onto my desk.

"Hmm?" he replied.

"I want to give my presentation," I said the words before the fear could beat me to it.

He lifted his head with a deep inhale and grinned. "I thought you might. Come on." He gestured out the door. I nodded timidly and followed him out.

"Oh and, Banana? I'm proud of you, with or without this." He squeezed my shoulder before bounding into the kitchen. He eagerly clapped his hands once, and Mom looked up from her conversation with Dad and Sugar. I felt everyone's eyes on me.

It was now or never.

Do or die.

Alexander the Great or Ana the Anonymous.

I thought for a moment but already could feel the words bubbling up inside of me.

"I'll do it," I said firmly.

Mom lit up with a smile and scurried over to squeeze my shoulders. "My brave girl," she said, brushing some of my messy hat hair from my cheeks.

Mom turned to Sugar. "Can we get a hand, Sugar? I think you'll be able to fix this much better than I would." She gave her a gentle smile and touched a hand to my puffy red eyes and face.

Sugar popped up from her chair and clapped her hands. "Ooh, you bet I can! I thought y'all would never ask!" She squealed and ran into the living room to grab her purse. She returned, brandishing a comb and several pots of makeup.

"Ana girl, you best be ready to sparkle!" she cried, grabbing my shoulders to shove me onto a chair.

It was go time.

Things You Can Always Count On:

1. Dads will do anything to keep their daughters from crying.

2. Moms will do anything to keep their daughters from not trying.

3. Grandfathers are never, *ever* what they seem. Even if you do have supposed "photographic evidence."

4. Women named Sugar, despite appearances and the fact that they may or may not be dating your grandfather, are excellent people to have around in a hair and makeup emergency.

chapter 17

"An electric eel can produce a shock of six hundred and fifty volts."

—*Animal Wisdom*

You know what else can produce a shock? The staring faces of every single person you've ever met, waiting for you to be amazing. Or worse, a complete idiot.

Bright sun warmed my already burning cheeks. The auditorium I would be speaking in wasn't far from the zoo house. It was outside, set up sort of like a small coliseum, with bleachers and a center ring with a gazebo for the presenter. Of course, now that I really looked at it, it reminded me of those rings where gladiators used to fight tigers while the audience taunted and laughed.

Fitting.

As we made our way there (and I checked my fly *and* my teeth), I put on my safari hat. No turning back now. The side braid that Sugar had somehow magically worked into my stubborn hair rested on my shoulder, boosting my confidence. She had also done wonders on my eyes and face, which were no longer puffy and red, but fresh-looking with a hint of sparkle. Even Mom liked it, and Mom is usually all "less is more" about makeup. If it weren't for the constant buzzing in my head, I might even say I looked good. Definite after picture.

Daz and Kevin took off to the back row of the bleachers, and Mom and Dad sat in the shade of the gazebo, which was set up with a small table. All of the reptiles I would be talking about were waiting quietly in their cages.

Paul, the director of education, emerged from behind an amplifier and gave me a small microphone that hooked onto my shirt. I could feel the eyes of the crowd on me but wasn't yet brave enough to face them. The constant hum of conversation poked away at my self-confidence as my heart skipped away in my chest.

Before I walked out onto the grass of the open auditorium, I peeked up from the gazebo to see who was there in the bleachers. Maybe I could find a few unfamiliar faces and hopefully focus on them, so I didn't wig myself out, right?

No such luck.

Front and center were the Sneerers. I wasn't surprised, but just the sight of them made my breathing speed up. Liv's voice echoed in my head, words that she hadn't said, but I needed to hear.

Relax. Breathe. You are smart, sophisticated, and special.

Zack was there too, on the far right of the bleacher. *Why did Zack have to come?* Like it wasn't bad enough to know he had totally heard me spew out his name on national television. He was smiling broadly at the Guy Who Wears Too Much Cologne and gawking at Sugar, who had taken a seat beside my mom with some of the other zookeepers. Obviously the guys were going to notice her—she *was* gorgeous—but did they have to snap pictures on their cell phones and jeer with each other? Gross.

I even spotted Rebecca and her friends in the crowd. That meant that actual eighth graders had come to see *me*. Beside them, a group of parents and two familiar, young, wide-eyed children shifted nervously, clearly keeping watch for another glimpse of the infamous caveman ghost.

I swallowed hard and looked for Bella. She was in the back row, next to Kevin and Daz. They all gave me quick thumbs-up. I swear, it felt like even the bugs in the air stopped flying so they could park themselves on a bleacher to gawk at me.

The buzz from the crowd began to drown out my mantra, and I soon noticed individual sounds. Little boys whined to their mothers and candy wrappers crinkled. My own feet made quiet treading sounds against the hot dirt. I could even hear the sound of someone watering the grounds in a neighboring exhibit. I'd read somewhere that in moments of sheer terror, people's senses got better—is that what was happening to me? *Did I have Spideysenses?*

I am smart, sophisticated, and special.

I looked over at my mom and grandpa, who were urging me to get out there. I took a step forward and tripped on the amplifier cord.

Oh, I was special all right.

Checking out the crowd one last time, I recognized Principal Miller, the math geeks, and even some of the drama kids. People I have barely talked to, but they showed up anyway. My stomach, which felt like I'd eaten a donkey earlier, suddenly felt empty and fluttery, like it had been taken over by a flock of bats. I stuffed my notes in my back pocket and stepped out into the sunlight.

Grandpa chose what he wanted to be, and so could I.

Breathe.

"Hello, everyone," I said, doing my best not to throw up during my first sentence. The crowd silenced, and I heard imaginary crickets for a moment. The crackling microphone on my lapel felt like an iron weight.

Keep going. Don't just stand there!

Then I noticed something: a *different* familiar face in the crowd.

Beatrix, the little girl that been my first audience, was waving at me frantically, bouncing up and down in her seat. Perched on her head was an oversized rugged hat, identical to mine, that she must have bought from the zoo shop. She was practically vibrating she looked so excited. Her mother, sitting beside her looking as well dressed as ever, gave me a quick smile and wave.

Then something happened. I don't know where it came from, and I couldn't help it.

I smiled back at her and waved.

The first part of my presentation was supposed to last around five minutes. I held my head high and began my introduction. Instead of looking at Zack's cocky smile or Ashley's sneer in the front row, I pretended like I was only talking to Beatrix.

"Today I'm going to be speaking to you about some of the reptiles here at the zoo." I sounded so loud on the sound system! I struggled to keep my voice clear and even.

"I'll start off with Goliath, who is our resident

boa constrictor," I said. My cheeks already stung from smiling so much. My hat did a good job of keeping the sun from my eyes, though.

Mom handed me the canvas bag that held Goliath, giving me a quick wink. I could tell she was already stoked that I hadn't made a run for it yet.

The crowd broke out into *oohs* and *aahs* as I reached into the bag and heaved out Goliath's sleek, wide body. I lifted him onto my shoulders with both hands and nestled him around my neck. The weight felt comforting actually, like he was a barrier between me and the crowd. I could hear a few shrieks from the audience as I tossed the empty bag to the side.

Hah! They were scared.

Walking back and forth across the center of the arena, I described Goliath. I had all of his stats down pat, thanks to my hours of rehearsal. He had also lived with us for a while at our other house when he was a hatchling. This was *so* much cooler than pretending in my room with a hairbrush iguana!

I kept sneaking peeks at Ashley, Brooke, and Rayna. Ashley looked like she was going to throw up all over their designer sandals, and Brooke was staring with wide eyes at Goliath. Rayna, who was holding onto a tiny camcorder, looked like she might pass out.

Awwwwe-some!

I continued to talk about Goliath, making sure to

move slowly so everybody could get pictures. When I had covered everything from my notes, I handed him to Dad, who nudged another open box toward me with his boot.

Otis.

I could tell the audience was eager to see what was next, so I took my time. Apart from the constant near-panic mode, I loved having the chance to make people squirm! I took my time collecting a large piece of carpeting from the table, noticing a nod of approval from Grandpa. He nudged my mom proudly.

"Now, this next reptile is Otis," I said, gingerly placing the carpet into the box and fitting it over the snapping turtle's two-foot shell. Using the carpet as a shield against Otis's snap-at-any-second jaws, I hoisted him from the box.

Another peal of emotion came from the crowd. I looked up at Zack for a moment, which was a big mistake. He was still joking around with Cologne Guy and watching Sugar. Ugh! Couldn't he pretend he was interested? Luckily, Otis raked a back claw against my pant leg and snapped me out of it.

Okay, focus.

I was almost done!

I set Otis down on the ground and began to describe him to the crowd. As I continued to talk, I made sure not to look at Zack again. I could tell my face was totally burning, but hopefully everybody thought it was the sun or something, and not random embarrassment and annoyance going full whack. I squinted up to Bella, Daz, and Kevin, who all gave me open smiles.

Finally, I reached the part of the presentation I was most dreading. My big finish with audience participation. I handed Otis to Mom and made my way toward the last crate.

With Otis now put away, the Sneerers had regained themselves. Ashley's glares stabbed at me, and they whispered back and forth. Before I could go back to ignoring them, a huge boulder seemed to fall in my stomach and my legs wavered. They were smirking, batting their eyes like they were swatting flies. Ashley pointed sneakily at the cameras to my left and right and whispered to Rayna.

A familiar feeling swept over me, not unlike that time in the cafeteria. Like how a lobster must feel in a tank at the supermarket. Ready to be picked up and cooked at any moment.

My eyes darted across the crowd. Nothing had changed. I sucked in a desperate breath, forcing myself not to bolt then and there. Had they planted someone to sabotage me? I was gritting my teeth at the rush of panic that had already taken over my body. Fear clamped down on my chest.

Something was up.

chapter 18

"The anaconda is the largest snake in the
world. They don't need venom. Instead
they are experts at ambushing prey."
— *Animal Wisdom*

The Sneerers kept smirking and whispering,
making out like they were waiting for something
huge to happen. Ashley kept sneaking looks at
Zack and giggling.

The audience started to shift in their seats; they
had noticed that I hadn't spoken in about a minute.
I wiped my sweaty palms on my thighs and looked at
the crowd. They had seemed so friendly a moment
ago; now I felt like they were a firing squad, eagerly
waiting for me to botch things up. I was the gladi-
ator now, waiting for the lion to come out so the
crowd could cheer as it tore me apart.

No! I bit my lip, searching frantically for a familiar

face, but all I could see was the growing smirk on Ashley's face.

As I stood there, no doubt looking utterly ridiculous and tongue-tied, she was winning. I knew it. She knew it. Zack knew it. Even the turtle probably knew it. All I could hear were muffled, panicked thoughts buzzing in my ears like a beehive as I felt the crowd start to cave in on me, ready to laugh at me for making a single mistake...

And then, something jerked me from my swarming thoughts. A bright flicker in the corner of my vision. Something round, something yellow.

A sunflower.

Brooke had reached into her pocket and pulled out her nail file, and was now staring at me with wide, assertive eyes. She looked down at the file in her hands and flipped it over in her palm, then back up at me. She wasn't filing her nails. She was just sitting there, holding it. Twirling it between her fingertips. What was it Brooke had said about that sunflower?

Then it dawned on me.

Focus.

Kevin had it right. They just wanted to mess with me so *I* screwed up on my own! They were way too cowardly to do anything. They wanted me to do it for them!

This was exactly what they wanted! To psyche me out!

I had depended on Liv practically every day of my life to help me fend off these snobby carnivores. And for years, they always won.

But Liv wasn't here anymore.

But that didn't mean I was alone.

I looked up at Daz, Bella, and Kevin, who were all grinning eagerly. I had friends. I had my parents. I had a famous grandpa and his sugary sweet girlfriend. I had the whole crowd in front of me, rooting for me.

And most importantly? I had that little seedling of bravery. The Sneerers would never change that, no matter what they did.

It was about time to show them.

I glimpsed back quickly at Mom, who was glaring something awful at Ashley. Then, in a moment that will go down in history as the apex of awesome *momitude*, she looked me straight in the eye, curled her lips into a smile, and gave me a devious nod.

I knew what I had to do.

I threw my hands on my hips and smiled at the crowd. I made sure to look directly into Ashley's perfectly lined eyes.

Because I had an idea, you see. I may be a total anonymous-social-reject-of-a-chicken-with-crickets-in-my-pocket, but I had something they didn't.

And I don't just mean the microphone.

I had Frankie.

Otherwise known as Louie's cousin. A young and feisty three-foot crocodile.

I glared back at Ashley. Think you can make me look like a total moron again? Not today, sweetheart.

I could still feel my pulse racing, but now, instead of slowing me down, it acted as a propeller. Ashley seemed unfazed by my realization and kept right on giving me the evil eye. Daring me to mess up. Rayna held the camera higher and giggled, her pink bangles clattering against each other on her wrist. Beside them, the tiny little sunflower was still perched in Brooke's hands.

I cleared my throat again and smiled.

I said, "Now, if someone wouldn't mind, I'm going to need a volunteer to help me with this next part. Someone who isn't afraid to get their hands dirty."

I could see Beatrix shoot her tiny hand in the air, but I had a better idea in mind.

I walked around the auditorium slowly, rubbing my hands together with anticipation. The audience was squirming in their seats—nearly everybody had their hand up. I squinted at the back row. Daz was beaming, shoving Kevin with excitement. Rebecca waved her hand eagerly and took a quick picture on her camera.

I knew what I wanted to do was against the rules—you weren't supposed to ask volunteers who didn't offer.

But still…

Brooke looked slightly unnerved, and Rayna was fidgeting with her purse, trying to avoid eye contact. Ashley had become enamored with the nail polish on her toes.

Not so brave now, were they?

I stopped in front of them and caught Brooke's eye, which darted beside her. I grinned at Ashley. "How about you?" I pointed at her.

Seriously, by the look on her face, I thought she was going to jump up right there and try to dropkick me. That is, if she hadn't been wearing flip-flops and a toe ring. She hesitated. Then, sticking her chin in the air, she said, "Ugh, *fine*."

"Are you afraid of crocodiles?" I asked. I made sure to look at the audience as I said it. Ashley flipped her hair and gave the audience a flirty smile.

"Absolutely not, *Scales*." She added that last part under her breath. A couple people in the front row chuckled, including Zack who had managed to tear his eyes off Sugar for ten seconds. But I didn't mind.

"Okay, great. Then you won't mind holding on to him for a second." I leaned down to pick up Frankie, carefully wrapping my hands around his shoulder and under his cream-colored belly. His mouth was tethered closed with a small band.

I held the young crocodile out to Ashley, enjoying the look of terror that was cracking through her mask of smirkiness.

"Do you mind?" I asked again, moving his scaled face closer to her. She jumped back, which caused a rift of laughter to roll through the crowd.

"You don't have to worry," I explained to the audience. I made sure to keep my voice slow and easygoing.

"Crocodiles have very strong muscles to close their jaws. But the muscles used to *open* them are very weak. He can't open his mouth as long as the band is on there." I pointed to the thick red band keeping Frankie's teeth where they belonged.

The color was draining from Ashley's face. I was still holding the crocodile out to her. I could see panic in her eyes: she was trying to figure out a way to get out of this and not look like a dork. She peeked up over at Zack, looking sheepish.

"I don't want to touch it," Ashley said quietly. She sounded annoyed, and she was scowling at me like a rabid hyena.

"You don't? Well, maybe our audience can give you a hand." I looked to the crowd as an invitation to clap. Daz was the first one, his hands shooting above his head in the back row.

Ashley glared at me one last time and slowly reached out her hands. I looked up at Rayna holding up her camcorder. She was still filming the entire thing.

I winked.

At first, I thought Ashley might drop the croc, turn right around, and sit back down. But she just stood there, with her lips all winched up like she was disgusted. I leaned in closer and handed Frankie over. He wasn't as heavy as he looked, but her arms trembled. For a second, I couldn't help but enjoy watching her panic. With Ashley twitching and staring at Frankie, I began to speak easily about his diet and natural history. Only a few minutes left!

Okay. I'll totally admit that I was completely happy with how this was going. I wasn't having a coronary like I expected, and the audience was totally engaged. And if Ashley hadn't been a tidal wave of social destruction for me during the past ten years, I might have even felt bad for her when it happened.

Or not.

I can't tell you why it did. Maybe the laughter of the audience had started to grow louder. Maybe it was the color of Ashley's hot magenta tank top, flashing in Frankie's eyes. Or maybe it was the bucketful of food that he'd eaten earlier. All I know is that it took one tremble from Ashley's outstretched arms to cause him to let loose.

That's right.

Right when I was nearing the end of my speech, as Ashley glared in disgust and threw me a furious look of "*you'll pay for this,*" Frankie decided he'd had enough.

By going to the bathroom.

All over her feet.

It was everywhere, covering her white sandals and manicured toes. And, okay, so crocodile pee isn't *that* gross, but it still smelled like an elephant farm on a hot day. I held my breath as I watched it happen.

Nobody in the crowd was prepared for the screech that flew out of Ashley's mouth faster than any insult she'd ever hurled at me.

Now, I've never seen *The Exorcist*—Mom won't let me watch it. But I can say that the moment the crocodile *went for it*, Ashley's face looked a *lot* like the preview that Liv and I had seen late that night on the Scream Channel. Her eyes were wide, and her eyebrows shot to her hairline. And what was worse (for her!) was that she couldn't put Frankie down until I took him back. It was like the gods had opened up the sky and offered me the most spectacular favor in the history of mankind. Or, at least, of junior high.

It was Grandpa that started to laugh first. The audience, who had been shocked into silence by her screech, began to join in; if a celebrity was allowed to laugh, then so were they. I looked up to see the laughing faces of Bella, Cologne Guy, Dad, and tons of other strangers in the bleachers. Rebecca even stood up, angling herself to take another picture of her sister covered in crocodile muck.

I turned to Ashley. She was white as an albino rabbit and was pleading at me with her eyes. I beamed at her, shrugging my shoulders to the crowd.

"Whoops! Looks like we had a little accident!" I nodded to the crowd, letting a big smile cross my face. I took Frankie from her, and she immediately ran off. Probably to find a bathroom. Rayna and Brooke stayed planted, but I couldn't help but notice Rayna followed Ashley with the camera. They really *were* programmed to follow her every move.

"There's a hose near the camel pen!" I shouted after her. Kevin was the first one to laugh this time, which filled my stomach with flutters of happiness.

The crocodile was still relaxing in my hands; I was pretty sure he was half-asleep by now. "Okay, anyone else like to give it a try at holding Frankie? Maybe we need someone big and strong here, seeing how this crocodile is pretty scary!" I raised my eyebrows at the audience, surprising myself with my strong voice.

A few guys in the back rows lifted their hands, including Daz, but it was Beatrix who jumped up in her seat and exclaimed, "*Me!*"

I nodded to her, inviting her to join me.

The last two minutes of my presentation were a blur. I didn't even mind when I noticed the cameraman zooming in on me; I even helped them get better views of Frankie. I managed to finish on time and even answer some questions about reptiles. One person even asked how I got so good at handling them!

When I was finally finished and turned back to the gazebo, my parents were waiting with Grandpa and Sugar.

"*Banana!* You were spectacular! A total natural." Grandpa picked me up and swung me around. If I hadn't been giddy as a cat on catnip already, I would have totally been embarrassed. But who cares? I'd done it, and not only did I do okay, I taught Ashley a lesson too!

"He's right, you know." Sugar giggled. "You were hotter than a Memphis sidewalk, girl!" She leaned in to hug me.

Now I knew how celebrities felt when they beat out other actresses for a role. I was like Angelina Jolie! Or Anne Hathaway! (Minus the awesome hair and scads of money and tanned thighs, because let's face it, that's not going to happen.) But outside of Hollywood, I felt like an absolute star. I took one last look at the crowd before they filed out, catching site of Ms. Fenton. Her soft-pink blouse stood out against her shiny hair. She waved to me before getting lost behind a throng of students.

Waving back, a teeny idea popped into my head. I still had until tomorrow night before her project deadline was up.

"Hey, Grandpa." I tugged on his shirt and pulled him aside. "Could you maybe do me a favor?"

He stood tall. "Anything you need, Banana."

"Think I could talk to your camera crew before they pack up? I…need their help with something important." I glanced behind me at the cameras, still trained on us. The feeling of being filmed didn't scare me anymore. For once, it just might save the day.

chapter 19

"An iguana can stay underwater for twenty-eight minutes."

—*Animal Wisdom*

KNOW what else can happen for twenty-eight minutes?! Paul, the zoo head honcho, talking to my parents about how awesome my presentation was! Seriously, my heart is going to fly out of my chest with a massive explosion of giddiness.

After letting Pete in on my plan (and after Rayna and Brooke took off to find a bathroom to reapply Ashley's ego and plot my demise, no doubt), Zack came up to me when I was talking to Beatrix. Did I mention that Bea said *she* wanted to work in a zoo when she was older? Because of *me*. So cool.

Anyway.

The funny thing about mothers is you can think they're so out of touch one minute, then the next they're totally eyeing you with that little knowing grin. Mom must have known something was going on when Zack sauntered up to me, because she kept giving me That Look. And when Dad kept on talking about turtle shells or something, she even grabbed him by the shoulder and said they had to get going.

"We have to check on the gorillas, hun, but you feel free to stay here and answer any more questions…" She trailed off, eyeing Zack suspiciously.

I shoved my hands in my pockets. For the first time in my life, I could look him in the eye without sputtering all over myself or struggling not to pass out. Had Sugar given me superpower makeup or something? Was it me?

"So, Annie," he said. I smiled, noticing that the familiar thumping in my chest had died away. I didn't even think about Ashley, who was probably staring daggers at me from someplace hidden.

"You were great out there today. It's totally awesome that you get to do this." He nodded his head, looking around the auditorium.

"Yeah, it took some getting used to"—I paused— "but I'm really glad I tried it." I was glad my mom didn't hear that.

He stood a little straighter and rocked on his heels. "So, do you have any more presentations coming up? I mean, are you busy tomorrow?"

I cocked my head.

He continued, "If you're not, I was thinking maybe you could come with me to the School End Dance? I know it's lame and probably isn't your thing, and maybe you've got something…maybe with Livia online, or…"

My face flushed, and I could hear a woodpecker in my chest. But the funny thing was, it wasn't a happy, excited woodpecker. It was a woodpecker that was warning me. A disappointed feeling floated up inside me. Sort of like when you finally go ahead and try a new kind of ice cream, only to realize that it wasn't worth all the hype. In fact, it wasn't worth ordering at all and you should have stuck with your favorite.

I chewed my lip. Hadn't Zack been making goo-goo eyes at Sugar the whole time anyways? Looking down at his hands, I noticed he was fiddling with a tennis ball, like he always did. A dark realization crept over me as I looked him in the eyes.

I couldn't believe I'd taken this long to figure it out.

"Zack," I said quietly, "was it you in the cafeteria?" I eyed him. "You know"—I pointed to his tennis ball—"with the chicken parm…all over me…" I emphasized each word.

His face went white, and he gave me a familiar look. It was the same look that Daz gave me when I caught him trying to put another cockroach in my boot or something equally awful. "You did! *You* were the one who threw it! Nobody has aim like that," I exclaimed, swatting the ball from his hand.

"Hey! Annie, I'm sorry! How was I supposed to know that you'd be some…" He stared at me, but his eyes darted to the camera crew that was packing up.

"What?! That I'd be on TV?! Or the news? You thought you'd show up now, right? Even though you've been as awful as the rest of them!" I gritted my teeth.

"So is that a no?" he muttered, scuffing the ground with his shoe.

"Maybe you should ask Ashley. I know she's wanted to go with you this whole year. It would make sense too, seeing how you're both attention-seeking jerks." I turned and stomped away, fuming at how stupid I could have been for all this time. How could he be so…arrogant?! Then I remembered something.

One last thing.

"Oh and, Zack?" I yelled, watching him swivel around with a moody look. It was so weird how he was cute this morning, but now he looked almost *boring* in his polo shirt. "My name is *Ana*!"

I stormed off behind the bleachers. I couldn't believe I just told off the guy I'd been crushing on forever. I also couldn't believe I'd been crushing on a total *dolt* forever, either. It felt like such a waste. I wanted to go back into all of my old notebooks and scribble over every time I mentioned his name. Especially the places where I'd smooshed together our names with a little heart around them. *Ugh*. Were all guys awful like that?

I huffed through my clenched teeth, squeezing my arms around my chest.

No, I knew they weren't.

Not all guys wore blazingly yellow polo shirts and tossed tennis balls into my chicken parm. Some stayed late at school for hours on a Friday night to help me with fractions. Some picked awful and degrading posters off the wall to protect me. Some, despite me being a total spaz on national television, would show up and cheer me on for the biggest day of my life so far.

"Ana?"

The voice was familiar as I felt a tap at my shoulder. I turned around and smiled.

"Hi, Kev." It's funny how I never noticed how pretty his hair color was until now. I was also suddenly ridiculously aware of his lips. His dark eyes.

"Quite the line up to get to you," he said, nodding

to the crowd. "I heard you tell off Zack." He grinned, revealing a small dimple on his cheek.

"Yeah…" I said, hoping that he couldn't hear my pulse going crazy. "He turned out to be a total jerk." I sighed.

Kevin stepped forward, making my vision tunnel. I had to work to stay balanced. "I was wondering if you'd ever figure that out."

"So are you going to the dance tomorrow?" I ventured, then immediately clamped my mouth shut. Why did I ask that? Of course he's not going to the dance. He's probably too busy building genius robots out of old Apple computers like the genius robot-building-Apple-computer guy he is, or maybe even going to some other dance at some other school with some other girl who does *not* have crickets in her pockets. He definitely wouldn't be going to some loser Monday-night dance where they serve watered-down fruit punch and—

"Yeah," he said, crossing his arms. "Daz wants to bring his Wolfman mask." He smiled knowingly. "Will I see you there?"

Oh.

I nodded, probably a little too eagerly. "Yeah. Maybe we should all go together." I fidgeted with the tip of my braid. "I mean, Bella and Daz and us two. We can get shakes before, maybe," I said.

He smiled, heaving a big exhale. "Awesome. I'll
see you tonight too. Daz and I are building a robot
tarantula at your place." His eyes twinkled.

Of course they were.

As I waved at him walking away, I had to steady
myself. It was like a dream. Better than a dream,
actually, because I didn't wake up to find any ancient
reptiles in my bed afterward. Before the presentation, I'd felt like the world had pecked little holes in
me—that the wind might blow me away. But now I
felt solid, like I could take on anything.

A paper airplane zoomed into my hair, poking me
in the ear.

Well, almost anything.

"Hey!" I didn't need to look to see who had
thrown it. Daz's eyes were narrowed. His hand was
stroking his chin like he had a beard. Like he was
capable of growing a beard. Hah.

"So…" he said, circling me like a shark. "You and
Kevin, hmm? Did I overhear something about a
dance?" He kept circling, eyeing me up and down. I
swung around to keep him from getting behind me.
Never turn your back on a sneaky sibling.

I stared at him, holding my chin high. A grin
leaked onto my face. "I don't know what you're talking about," I prompted him. I tapped the brim of
my hat up with a flick of my finger. "We're all going

together. Including Bella," I said. "I didn't think *you'd* have any complaints," I said slyly. "Or maybe I should tell her that you don't want to go…?" I trailed off, pretending I was looking around for Bella.

He squared his shoulders at me, and I readied myself for the noogie that was inevitably coming. Good-bye, beautiful side braid. His eyes were narrow slits of gray, but he couldn't hide the grin either. I knew what my own bluff face looked like just as well as his. And he knew it.

"I suppose I can deal with it," he said but still gave me a halfhearted shove in the arm. When you have a brother, you learn the language of his shoves pretty quickly, and this one said, "Thanks, brat."

He so owed me.

"But maybe we should all do dinner instead of shakes," he said with a sneaky grin.

"Oh, sure," I scoffed. "Because I'm loaded with lots of money from my big movie scene." I poked at the pathetic bits of lint balled inside my pocket.

"I'll pay." He shrugged, giving me a false look of innocence. He looked like he might burst if I didn't ask him what the heck he was up to.

"Do I even want to know?" I grimaced.

"I might happen to have a little extra money this year," he said loftily, crossing his arms. "I thought it would be a nice gesture as a *brother*, you know? Take my sister and her friends out to dinner…" His voice was low and oh-so-proud. Totally devious Daz at his finest.

"Did you *steal* from somebody?" I asked. I searched the auditorium for someone looking for a missing wallet. Mom would have his butt grounded for life. "Ohh, you are so going to get it!"

His mouth fell open in mock disbelief. "Of course not. What do you think I am? An amateur? I've merely been providing a unique zoological *experience*," he said.

"Meaning…?" A vision of the bags of crickets that he'd snuck from the kitchen bubbled up in my mind. The crowds of visitors outside my window every morning.

"I've been letting some lucky zoo-goers feed my snakes, that's all."

My jaw dropped. "People have been *paying* you to do your own chores?!" I shrieked. My own brother. Either the biggest con in the world or, I hated to admit, a supergenius.

His eyes brightened, and he checked behind him for any signs of Mom. "Brilliant, right?" he said, nudging me with an elbow.

"Thirty percent or I tell Mom." I lifted my chin. Clearly he was a bad influence on me. "*And* no more snakes in my bed. Ever."

He gave me an appraising stare. "Ten," he replied, his eyes twinkling. "And no dice on the snakes."

Some things will never change. "Fine, twenty."

"Done," he said, spitting on his hand and holding it out to me. I considered for a second before giving in, slapping my hand into his gooey palm. What's the phrase? If you can't beat 'em, join 'em?

I'd have to warn Bella about him, for sure.

I looked toward the tent at my new friend, who was, in a totally bizarre image, talking excitedly to Kevin in the bleachers.

I felt a swell of pride bubble up inside me as I watched.

I, Ana Wright, had done it. I led my presentation, finished seventh grade with a bang (well, more like a splat—hah!), landed my first group date (it counts!), and felt *amaaaz-ing*.

So what if my entire family lived in a zoo and I smelled like every stinky animal known to man.

So what if my best friend lived on the other side of the planet with sheep and hobbits.

So what if my grandpa is a world-renowned crazy naturalist with a girlfriend named after a food group.

And so what if I have a ridiculous safari hat on my head.

Actually, the hat totally sucks. But still.

chapter 20

"Crocodiles don't have sweat glands and must release heat through their mouths."
—*Animal Wisdom*

Art project deadline: T-minus thirty minutes.

Hurry up, Ana.

I squirted a thin line of glue on the last photograph and searched for one last empty spot on the poster board. The stills that Pete had given me from my presentation were perfect. I was in some of them, holding Goliath, Otis, and Frankie for the audience to see. My side braid was shiny in the sunlight, and I couldn't help but giggle when I saw the happy twinkle in my eyes. I was teaching a whole crowd of people, and that giddy feeling hadn't left me all weekend. Like I was a kite flying on the wind.

But my new seventh-grade true self collage was a lot more than just me.

The faces of Mom and Dad were tucked in around the colorful animal photographs, along with Grandpa in his bright shirt and Sugar in her ginormous heels and perfect miniskirt. Daz's sneaky grin, Kevin's dimple, and Bella's hair clips stood out against the lime-green poster board. Even the Sneerers, hiding behind a picture of a camel, were there. I figured that I wouldn't be my seventh-grade true self without them, so why not include *everybody*, right? Magazine cutouts of banana splits, old pictures of Liv clinging to me at our sixth-grade graduation, and my grandpa's newspaper article peppered the borders. In the center was a tiny seedling I'd painted in bright green.

I stuck the last photo down.

"What do you think, Darwin?" I held the poster up so Darwin could see where I'd placed him, snug against a picture of me joking with Daz. "This is my true seventh-grade self."

Darwin whistled. "Ana banana! Iguana banana!" He bebopped on his perch, sending a spray of sunflower seeds to the floor. A few bounced under my bed. I knelt down carefully, trying not to mess up my dress. I have to admit, having Sugar around to help me get ready for the dance was a major plus. She even did my hair in a classy updo that she said made me look fourteen! I think she was right because Dad looked like he was going to faint when he saw me all dressed up. Making sure my hair wouldn't catch on the bottom of my bed, I leaned over and grabbed the sunflower seeds. My last project, crumpled against some socks, peeked out at me. The dark, jagged lines and animal pictures were crumpled at the edges. Compared to the colorful collage I'd just finished, my old project looked pretty bad.

"Gross," I said, pulling it out.

"Blech! Ew!" Darwin chimed in. I couldn't help but agree. I started to throw it away, but something stopped me. A stomach-swirly-niggly feeling. I mean, the project *was* supposed to be about our seventh-grade true self. But what if your true self was more than one thing?

I laid the two projects side by side. Black and white against colorful and bright. I knew what I had to do.

Grabbing a piece of paper, I scribbled a note.

Dear Ms. Fenton,

I know you said we were supposed to show you

our seventh-grade true selves with this project. But I have a feeling my true self is a lot of things. I WANT to be like the second collage. I feel bright and happy when I'm teaching people about animals. But sometimes it's hard to be your true self. And sometimes, I think our true self hides behind other things and comes out a little messed up, like the first collage I gave you. I've thought about it, and I think the "true" self is whatever one I choose to be. So I wanted you to have both projects. Together, I think they sum up my seventh-grade true self. Thanks for being a great teacher and giving me a chance to get this to you. Oh, and if you still want to display it for the students next year, I'm okay with that. ☺

Love, Ana

I stacked the posters together. Sticking the note to the side with a paperclip, I smoothed on some chocolate lip gloss and checked myself in the mirror one last time.

Hair? Perfect.

Dress? Not too short, with just the right amount of swooshy-ness at the bottom when I spun around.

Shoes? Teensy tiny heels that I could actually *walk* in, with two butterflies studded to the strap.

I grinned at the thought of taking a little animal reminder with me to the dance.

"Bye, Darwin!" I giggled. "Wish me luck!"

"Ana banana!" He chirped as I tucked my project under my arm and bounded down the stairs.

Outside, I had to dodge the nosy pelicans. The smell of hippos was still strong in the hot summer air as I hopped into the truck where Mom, Bella, Daz, and Kevin were waiting. Teeny red flowers that matched her dress studded Bella's hair, and Kevin looked completely adorable in his suit. Daz was even wearing a tie. Okay, so it had cartoon snakes on it, but it was totally him.

"Ready to go to your first dance?" Mom squeezed my arm as she drove past the lion exhibit.

"You bet," I said.

And I was.

My summer stretched ahead of me like a blank, open notebook, and for the first time, I couldn't *wait* to fill it up.

ANA AND LIVIA'S HALF-BIRTHDAY HOMEMADE CHOCOLATE LIP GLOSS

In case you ever want to make your own half-birthday lip gloss, follow these steps!

STUFF YOU'LL NEED:
- Vaseline (you can get this supercheap at any pharmacy or drugstore.)
- Cocoa powder
- Small, microwave-safe bowl
- Spoons
- Microwave
- Small containers for your lip gloss (I like using jars with twisty tops. You can get these at craft or beauty supply stores.)
- Stickers or labels (for decorating your finished lip gloss!)

WHAT TO DO:
1. Add a big spoonful of Vaseline to the microwave-safe bowl. You don't have to be too specific for this recipe, so just glob some in!

2. Microwave the Vaseline for about two minutes. Watch it carefully so it doesn't boil! When it's melted, *carefully* take the bowl out. Use oven mitts and don't burn yourself!

3. Add a small spoonful of cocoa powder to the Vaseline and begin mixing. You can add as much as you like. Remember: the more cocoa powder you add, the darker the tint will be. Stir the chocolate-goop mixture to make sure there are no cocoa powder lumps.

4. Return the bowl to the microwave for another ten to twenty seconds. Stir it again.

5. Get your lip gloss containers ready and spoon in the mixture. Let it cool in the container. Soon it will be smooth with a shiny finish!

6. Use stickers or labels to decorate your lip gloss. That's it! Your lips will smell like hot chocolate, so pucker up!

acknowledgments

Writing a book is like wrangling a crocodile; you just can't do it unless you have help with the scary bits. If I had my way, you'd all get a chapter of thanks!

First of all, to Kathleen Rushall. There are no words to express how grateful I am to have you as my brilliant agent and friend. Your unwavering patience, wisdom, and humor mean the world to me. This one's for you too.

To Aubrey Poole and the rest of the amazing team at Sourcebooks for giving Ana the perfect home. Your keen eyes, heart, and enthusiasm are on every page.

To Liv (the real one), Alina, Adrienne, Carter, and the rest of my friends in the kid lit community who cheered me on every step of the way. I owe you all ice cream sundaes!

To all the incredible teachers and librarians out there, especially those who gave me extra books to read.

To my family, and to Mom and Dad for never complaining about the zoo they lived in.

To Justin, for all the love and laughter.

And finally thank *you*, dear reader! May you always be your truest self. Even if it gets you covered in crocodile muck.

about the author

Jess Keating was nine years old when she brought home a fox skeleton she found in the woods and declared herself Jane Goodall, and not much has changed since then. Her first job was at a wildlife rehabilitation center, where she spent her days chasing raccoons, feeding raptors (the birds, not the dinosaurs!), and trying unsuccessfully to avoid getting sprayed by skunks. Her love of animals carried her through college, where she studied zoology and received a master's in animal science, before realizing her lifelong dream of writing a book for kids about a hilarious girl who lives in a zoo.

She has always been passionate about three things: writing, animals, and education. Today, she's lucky enough to mix together all three. When she's not writing books for adventurous and funny kids, she's hiking the trails near her Ontario home, watching documentaries, and talking about weird animal facts* to anyone who will listen. You can email her at jesskeatingbooks@gmail.com, or visit her online at www.jesskeating.com.

*Did you know a sea cucumber breathes out its butt?

CREATURE FILE:
Jess Keating

SPECIES NAME: Authorificus Biophiliac

KINGDOM: Ontario, Canada!

PHYLUM: Writers who have a strange love of quirky critters and brave characters; Animal nut with a pen.

WEIGHT: You dare ask a lady her weight?! Why, I never! Wait, is this before or after I ate that banana split?

NATURAL HABITAT: Outside exploring with a messy notebook or snuggled up watching nature documentaries with her husband.

FEEDS ON: Grilled apple and cheese sandwiches, popcorn, and pizza.

LIFESPAN: I was born on a sunny summer day in... wait, nobody has time for my life story here. Get it together, Jess.

HANDLING TECHNIQUE: Gets restless inside, so daily walks are essential. Also have significant quantities of caramel corn and extra books on hand in case of emergency.

HOW TO
OUTSWIM
A
SHARK
WITHOUT A
SNORKEL

Book 2 in the
My Life is a Zoo series

COMING JANUARY 2015

After becoming the zoo's most popular student ambassador, Ana Wright is starting to love her life. But when her famous grandfather funds a new aquarium, Ana's life goes from sunny to sunk.

Now Ana's stuck working with Ryan (the younger brother of the cute marine biology student) all summer—and he's the biggest PAIN Ana has ever met. With confusing new boys, old enemies, and even more animal poop in her life, Ana's newest adventure has her questioning why, after finally getting her life sorted out, do things have to change again?

Read on for a sneak peek!

chapter 1

"Some sharks can never stop moving, or else they will suffocate and die."

—*Animal Wisdom*

Hijinx at the Zoo? August 20th

Visitors to the Zoo this Sunday got a big surprise when Ana Wright, granddaughter of the famed Shep Foster, fell into a shark tank during an educational presentation. The twelve-year-old wasn't injured.

"It looked like she just threw herself in!" said Jonathon Wexley, a local business owner who witnessed the accident. "One minute that other girl was talking about sharks, and the next? She just jumped!" The impromptu dip in the shark tank wasn't the only surprise that day, when police arrived at the scene to arrest...

One month earlier.

Throwing myself into a shark tank is *not* my idea of a good time. Luckily, my summer didn't *start* with sharks. But it did start with some big changes.

No. Big is an understatement.

Ginormous.

Uber.

Behemoth.

It also started with snorkels.

It's funny how you can blink and your entire life is different. One minute you think things will stay the same for a while. Then right when you get used to them, they go changing again just to mess with you. This is why I was so against this whole snorkeling thing from the get-go.

I took a huge breath and dipped under the water again, feeling the panic hit me like an ice cold wall.

I can do this. I'm not going to drown. Nope. Except it's really hard to do those deep, cleansing breaths underwater.

In. I tried to suck in a breath.

Out. The *whoosh* of air was loud in my ears, fake and rattling.

A toddler and his mother splashed by me, sending a trail of goose bumps snaking up my legs. The blurry outlines of a nearby peacock moved above me, strutting around on the lookout for tossed french fries at the edges of the water. Underwater, the hard, gritty floor of the pool was digging into my knees.

The sound of my heart pounding in my ears began to drown out the splashes.

Shoot.

I'd forgotten to breathe again.

I tried to suck in a breath, but the mask on my face stopped me from getting any air. I couldn't breathe. I *couldn't breathe*!

"Don't breathe through your nose!" Grandpa bellowed as I lurched my head up from the water. Daz slapped me on the back as I choked, hacking up a mouthful of cold, stinging water. My hair was stuck against my face like sloppy, wet tentacles.

"I can't get it!" I wailed. "Why is this so *hard*?!" I yanked the mask from my face and squished my cheeks. The rubbery-suction had left lines on my skin that hurt to touch. Grandpa gave me a sympathetic look, but my brother just shook his head and splashed me. A few other families in the wave pool turned to stare at me, like I was an angry seal causing a scene.

"It's not hard," Daz laughed. "It's just *breathing*! You do it all the time! In! Out! Repeat!"

Ugh.

Figures that I could mess up something as simple as *breathing*. What happened to my super-fun-no-worries-awesome summer, huh? I watched as Daz stuffed his snorkel into his mouth and slipped under the water again. Water slopped off his hand as he pointed dramatically to the top of his snorkel and loudly breathed the air in and out.

"Show off," I muttered. I aimed a kick at his mask under the water, but missed and slipped on the gritty floor of the pool. It is impossible to stay ticked off when you have water up your nose. I hated swimming. Well, okay. That isn't exactly true. I don't mind *standing* in water, splashing around. But actually going underwater? I'd rather face off against an angry croc than go underwater. There's no air under there, you know. This is why if I have a choice to swim or stay on firm land, I pick land every single time. That and this horrible swimsuit of mine that digs into my shoulders like nobody's business and rides up my butt...but that's another story.

Last week Grandpa announced that he wanted us to learn how to snorkel. Ever since he came to visit a while ago, it's been one project after another and it is beyond tiring. He burst into the house carrying a bunch of swimming masks and snorkels. "It's like living in another world!" he'd said. "Like an alien planet! A skill that everyone should have!"

Blah, blah, blah.

If it's a skill that *everyone* should have, then

wouldn't we be born with gills in our necks? He didn't seem to think that was funny, though.

Why did we have to learn *now*, when summer is already super busy with zoo stuff and generally lazing about NOT going to school? I have no idea.

All I know is that he was super secretive about it, saying it was "about time" and that it's part of some "big surprise" that he keeps hinting at. Grandpa could be hard to handle at the best of times, what with the paparazzi following him and all, but this was much worse. Turns out having a secret made him *extra* cheerful.

My brother Daz was psyched to learn how to snorkel, but I didn't want to admit that the idea of submerging my head and trying to *breathe* underwater seemed completely unnatural and would probably be the death of me. That's no surprise. You can pretty much guarantee that if it's insane, Daz will be up for it. Of course, most people don't learn to snorkel in the wave pool at the zoo surrounded by wandering peacocks, but that's what you get when you're me and you live in a zoo.

"You did great for today, Banana," Grandpa said, sloshing out of the pool. I hauled myself out of the water before Daz could splash me again. The feeling of failure dripped over me, running in trails down my skin along with the water. We'd been trying for days already, and I still couldn't get it. "You'll figure this soon enough, it's just a matter of training your brain to not panic with the snorkel." He checked his watch. "I have to go check on something. Why don't you go home and dry off and meet me in half an hour by the polar bear tank? Don't forget!"

I nodded, my insides clenching with nerves. "And I'll finally get to hear about this giant surprise, right?" I couldn't keep the sarcasm out of my voice. Last time he surprised us I ended up on TV. I was *not* ready to relive that little shenanigan.

"You got it!" He gripped Daz by the shoulder and yanked him away. "Come with me, young man. You can help an old man out."

I giggled, watching Daz try to keep up with Grandpa. He may be older, but Grandpa can still dodge a rattlesnake when he needs to. Which is pretty often, really. Families hushed as they walked past, and a few cameras clicked as "the famous Shep Foster" gave them a wide smile. He was *good* at being in the spotlight, that was for sure.

I took another big gulp of warm air, happy that I didn't have to breathe through that straw anymore. Whatever Grandpa's surprise was, I hoped breathing normally was part of the plan.

"Hey, it's her!" A girl's voice sounded muffled in my waterlogged ears. "It's Ana Wright! That's her! *Hey, Ana!*"

I brushed the hair out of my face to see two young girls rushing toward me. They waved frantically, while their mother snapped a picture. "Can we get a picture with you?" Their flip-flops slapped against the ground as they hopped in place.

My breath caught in my chest as I straightened up. *Not with this hair! Not in this swimsuit!* I panicked, but the smiles on their faces were infectious. I wrapped my towel closer around my chest.

"Sure," I said, waving them over. *Just be cool.* I ran my fingers through my hair, trying to fluff it up so I didn't look like a wet mop, and tried to force my shoulders straight. I wished for the zillionth time that I looked more like Sugar, my Grandpa's superhot actress girlfriend.

The girls looked about six or seven, both with shiny red cheeks from the hot sun. A green bag overflowing with gift shop stuffed animals was slung over their shoulders, and their zoo T-shirts were baggy on them. A stab of jealousy nagged at me. Life was so *simple* when you were a little kid. Not like the nonsense I have to put up with.

"We loved your presentation last month! I want to be you for Halloween this year! I got a hat from the gift shop and *everything*!" The girl with strawberry blond hair was practically panting she was talking so fast. She dug into her bag and pulled out the crumpled hat, tugging it onto her head. "How cool is it that you're going to be in an actual *movie*?!"

I smiled for another shot, but felt the strain in my cheeks. "More like a documentary," I said, gripping my nails into my palm. "But it is definitely crazy!"

There's an understatement.

It had been a few weeks since I'd been a part of a media circus at the zoo, but I was still getting recognized by some people. This is one of those ginormous changes I was talking about, and boy, was it taking some getting used to. Getting recognized in school is one thing. But just out wandering around the zoo? That's some Level 10 bizarro right there.

"Is it true that you're named after an anaconda? And that you're the youngest presenter here?!" The one with black hair stared at me with wide eyes. She lowered her voice. "I read that online," she gushed. Her friend nodded wildly.

I tried not to cringe. "Y…yes." I said. A month ago I wouldn't be caught dead admitting that, but they both beamed.

"We know everything about you," she said solemnly.

Yikes.

"What's with all the construction signs?" They gestured to the roped off area beyond the polar bear tank. "Are you getting some new animals? *Ooh!* Are they going to be part of your next presentation?! Are they pandas?! I *so* hope they're pandas!" They were bouncing again on their heels.

I backed away slightly. All that energy was hard to handle, you know? Like they were little bugs about to land all over me.

"Uhh," I said. "I don't actually know. It's been really busy this summer so far, but I don't know if we have any new animals coming." I admitted. "It's a lot of work to get new creatures here, so it only happens after a *lot* of planning."

"Ohhh," they said. My hair was dripping water down my back now, which was freezing cold against my hot skin. I glanced up to their mom hopefully.

"All right, girls," she said, smiling gently. "Let's not take up too much of her time. She probably wants to get dried off and enjoy the rest of her day!" She coaxed the girls away as I waved thankfully.

"Bye!" They waved one last time as they left, chattering on the way.

I wrapped the towel tighter and started to walk home, marveling at how much my life had changed.

"Well, Darwin? Any ideas what this big surprise of Grandpa's is? If you've overheard something *now* is the time to tell me." I stuck a raisin through the bars of the cage on my floor, peering in to see his glittery black eyes. Darwin is my African grey parrot, and despite being a total loudmouth he's one of my best friends. He even lets me practice my presentations in front of him, and only gets excited when I talk about reptiles. You should have seen his face when I told him that he's related to dinosaurs. Total drama queen.

He ruffled his feathers and picked away at the raisin, ignoring me.

"Thanks for all the help." I rolled my eyes at him before I bounded down the stairs and slammed the front door of the research house that was our home for the summer.

Luckily the polar bear tank was close, just beyond the lion pen. I didn't know what I was expecting to see when I got there, but I *really* wasn't expecting to see my whole family.

"Mom! Dad!" I called as they milled about, looking about as confused as I felt. "What are you doing here?" I checked around us for cameras, but no suspicious cameramen were nearby. Honestly, it's like Grandpa *liked* messing with my nerves.

Mom whipped around. Her hair was messy, frizzing out around her hat. "Ana! We've been just waiting for you. Dad wouldn't start without you." She gave me a look that told me she was just as on edge about all this. The back of her zoo uniform was stained with perspiration.

"What's this all about?" I asked. I was almost afraid to hear the answer. Grandpa noticed me and clapped his hands together. Sugar stood beside him in her usual miniskirt and heels, wriggling with excitement.

"We're all here!" He cleared his throat, and I could tell a speech was coming on. Grandpa *loved* to have everyone's attention. A few zoo visitors milled around, staring inquisitively. "As you know, I've been planning a little something as a surprise." He turned to look at Mom. "Janie, you remember that summer we spent on that fishing boat? When you were six or seven?"

Mom nodded with recognition, but she was still suspicious. Her hand gripped mine tighter. "Yes…"

Grandpa smiled. "Well, I've been thinking, a little time at sea should be mandatory for all kids." He gestured widely, with a faraway look in his eyes.

I did not like where this was going.

"Dad…" Mom said. Her voice was low. "What did you do? You know we can't send the kids on some boat right now."

Boat?! Who said anything about a BOAT?!

"Mom…?" I said, panicked. I squeezed my nails into her hand, telepathically communicating my terror. Beside me, Daz was practically bouncing out of his skin.

Grandpa shook his head. "No, no, no," he said. "There's no boat this time, although that *would* be a great plan." Sugar nodded sagely, but kept her lips pursed.

Already I was feeling seasick.

"*But*, I did manage to wrangle some resources together. *Secretly.* Which is very hard to do around here, I'll have you know." He winked and led us toward the construction signs behind him.

Dad glanced nervously at me, tugging at his mustache. We followed behind Grandpa slowly, like he might lead us into a lion's den. Which, knowing him, he totally would do.

"And I'm very happy to report that it has been a success. We're not completely finished with the renovation, but we're going to go public soon. I just wanted you to know first, before Sugar and I leave for Los Angeles tomorrow," Grandpa said.

"Know what, Shep?" Dad said. Always the voice of reason. His eyebrows were scrunched together and his mustache was twitching.

"Glad you asked, Henry," he said, waving us closer. He threw open the plastic tarp around the pavilion door and we all stepped inside. The first thing that hit me was the cool air.

Well, that and the fishy smell.